VIVA, ROSE!

VIVA, ROSE!

SUSAN KRAWITZ

Holiday House / New York

Copyright © 2017 by Susan Krawitz
All Rights Reserved
HOLIDAY HOUSE is registered in the U.S. Patent
and Trademark Office.
Printed and bound in March 2017 at Maple Press, York, PA, USA.
Photo of Pancho Villa & staff, Library of Congress, Prints & Photographs Division,
LC-DIG-ggbain-29882
Front page of *The San Antonio Light* with "Around the Plaza" column by Jeff Davis,
March 9, 1932 © San Antonio Express News/Zuma. Image courtesy of Ancestry.com.
www.holidayhouse.com
First Edition
1 3 5 7 9 10 8 6 4 2

Library of Congress Cataloging-in-Publication Data

Names: Krawitz, Susan, author.
Title: Viva, Rose! / by Susan Krawitz.
Description: First edition. | New York : Holiday House, [2017] | Summary: In El Paso,
Texas, in 1915, thirteen-year-old Rose Solomon seeks her missing
brother's return and inadvertently ends up running with Pancho Villa and
his revolutionary army.
Identifiers: LCCN 2016034882 | ISBN 9780823437566 (hardcover)
Subjects: LCSH: Villa, Pancho, 1878-1923—Juvenile fiction. | CYAC: Villa,
Pancho, 1878-1923—Fiction. | Revolutionaries—Fiction. |
Prejudices—Fiction. | Jews—United States—Fiction. | El Paso
(Tex.)—History—20th century—Fiction.
Classification: LCC PZ7.1.K736 Vi 2017 | DDC [Fic]—dc23 LC record available at
https://lccn.loc.gov/2016034882

*This book is dedicated to my daughter
Hannah Munson and her cousin Rose Ajemian,
my family's current crop of feisty,
fabulous redheads.—S.K.*

Chapter 1.

It's a good thing I saw that newspaper before Papa and Momma did.

It lay on the counter of Pickens Mercantile for all of El Paso to see, with a photograph blazed across its front under the words THE SOUTHWESTERN SCOURGE OF 1915!

The picture showed a group of men staring squint-eyed at the camera, nearly every one of them decorated with scraggly whiskers and a wide Mexican hat. Below it was written "The notorious gang of Mexican outlaw Pancho Villa, known also as La Cucaracha."

They were a gang of roughnecks, that much was plain, and right in their middle stood the roughest of them all—a round-jawed man with a brushy moustache and a gaze so hard his eyes looked boiled. The fellow to his left didn't seem quite as fierce, though he had a face full of whiskers, some kind of belts crisscrossed on his chest, and he clutched a gun as big as the branch of a tree. His hair covered his forehead, but I didn't need to see a wide birthmark to know to the bottom of my soul I was looking at the face of my brother Abraham.

I'm not prone to fits like my mother, but I began to shiver as if I'd swallowed ice. My face went burning hot, and when I raised my hands to my forehead I must have banged against the molasses jar Mr. Pickens keeps next to the newspapers.

The lid fell off and it toppled right over, and though the jar was only half full, enough molasses oozed out to cover nearly every *bandido* on the page in sticky goo.

Mr. Pickens was terribly sharp with me.

"Stand away, girl!" he cried, and tried to push the stuff off the paper with a cloth. He threw the rag to the floor, then turned to my father and said, "Do you see what that child of yours has done?"

My mother started to pull at the cuffs of her dress, like she does when she is embarrassed. "If you'd been, for once, acting like a lady...," she hissed, but Papa just raised an eyebrow and smiled at me with the half of his mouth Mr. Pickens couldn't see.

"Rose!" he said, sounding nearly serious. "You've ruined the news!" Then he added in Yiddish (but sternly, so it sounded like real scolding), "Don't worry about it, my *shayna*. It's only paper, not the czar's jeweled eggs."

Momma sighed loudly and positioned a hand on her forehead like an actress in the moving pictures. Papa turned back to Mr. Pickens and said in English, "A simple mistake."

Mr. Pickens gathered the coins Papa pushed across the counter, and shook his head in my direction. The money wasn't enough to take the fire from his tongue.

"It was not an ordinary newspaper she destroyed—it was my last copy with a picture of that thieving La Cucaracha! I was fixing to post it right there," he said, and he aimed his pointing finger at the posters of rough-faced outlaws on the wall behind him. "But now any one of those Mexican villains can saunter in and ask for hair cream and horehound candy, and I won't know I'm living my last day until I feel the steel of his knife at my throat!"

Mr. Pickens apparently had a dramatic streak to rival Momma's.

"I'm very sorry, sir," I said. I bobbed my head at him in a way he might think was a curtsy, then turned and fled to the back of the store. I stopped by a bolt of calico. *Thump, thump, thump.* The walls echoed with the loud beats of my heart.

My brother with that gun, shoulder to shoulder with a "notorious outlaw" called La Cucaracha? I had heard the youngest children at school singing a song about a *cucaracha*, a word that sounded too pretty to attach to anyone in that photograph, including Abraham.

One of my hair ribbons fluttered to the floor. My hands were shaking so hard I could barely twine my unruly ginger strands back into a braid.

Abe's secrets. That's what was making me burn and freeze, and working at rattling me to pieces. Until Abe made me keep them, I'd only in my life withheld one truth from my parents, about the time Mr. Pickens's mother pressed two sweets into my hand and charged me for just one.

Abe's secrets were a far bigger freight, and they'd been

weighting my sleep by night and crowding my thoughts by day. He had lied, lied, lied to our parents—told them one thing, and gone to do another. He was off to visit our brother Eli, who was working in the eastern city of Brooklyn, where Papa's relations lived. That's what he'd told us four months before. But then I found a letter Eli had sent him. *"Your secret is safe with me,"* Eli wrote. *"I will support the ruse."* Of course, I told Abe I'd read it. Who wouldn't? And he confessed to me the real truth. Abe was not heading east at all, but farther west. He was setting off to herd cattle and ride horses across the open range.

But the photograph I saw in the newspaper revealed that the heavy load I'd been carrying for my brother was not the real truth at all.

Abraham hadn't left us to become a cowboy. He'd gone off to be a low-life bandit in a cowboy hat.

Chapter 2.

Another secret my brother cursed me with was that he had a sweetheart, the dainty Miss Polly Brunckhorst, who was my teacher and also the so-called love of his life. And that's who I thought of as I stood in the back of Pickens's store. Abe had revealed to her his cowboy plans, and the fact that I knew of them too. Soon after he left, Miss Polly found a way to send him letters, and so I'd written a few and gotten one back—a two-page dispatch about life on the open range. I treasured that letter. How sad it now seemed that it had just been a badly scrawled lie.

Poor Miss Polly. She deserved to know the truth about where Abe had really gone. She would be shocked and horrified at the news. Furious too, most likely.

I could barely wait to tell her.

But leaving the store without asking permission would surely bring Momma's reproach my way. She and Papa didn't seem to be in much of a hurry to go. In fact, they were still standing by the counter, listening patiently as Mr. Pickens let loose a scour of hot words.

He was working up an agitation as fierce as those politicians who had parked themselves in front of the bank last autumn, and talked election gibberish until the sun set. "They say they're fighting because they're tired of gettin' bossed around by the rich folk—well, I call that plain foolishness," Mr. Pickens was saying. "It's just an excuse for thievin' and killin' and bloody lawlessness."

Mr. Pickens seemed to possess a deep well of critical opinion, but he became especially unkind when he discussed people from Mexico. They numbered many in our town because the country lay just south of us, separated from El Paso only by a river called the Rio Grande. My friends Elsa and Gabriela had been born in that place, and Mr. Pickens's rantings always made me wonder if he would talk ill of me, as well, if he knew they were my companions.

Mr. Pickens aimed his pointing finger toward the ceiling and shook it. "They'll get old Black Jack Pershing's army after them soon enough. He'll clean their Mexican clocks and throw whatever's left of them in jail to rot." I couldn't imagine what the Mexican folks' clocks had to do with this, but he spoke the words with mean-spirited triumph.

My father said something in reply, but not loud enough for me to hear. The more angry Papa gets, the quieter his words come. "Speak up, man!" Mr. Pickens said crossly. "Hard enough to understand your kind of people as it is."

My father tried again, and this time his voice came

clearly. "If you have never known bondage," he said, "then you cannot know how great a gift is freedom."

Mr. Pickens's response was a snort.

"Them uprising Mexicans don't got the brains or sense to know the difference between freedom and slavery," he said. "Their landowners been taking care of 'em all these years and helping 'em run things proper. You'd think they'd show a half ounce of grateful."

I heard the jingle of coins, and my father's voice came once more, so low now it was almost a growl. "Yes," he said. "In Russia, that is what the government told our people as well."

I heard the creak of the door's hinges. "Come, Rose!" Papa called, and I followed him into the glaring relief of sunshine.

Momma was clutching the tin of tooth powder we had come in to buy. "I tell you again, Sol," she said, "do not speak of the old country. We were treated badly there, and that is why we left. Here, all is different. We can do as we please, shop where we want, walk about as we wish. But remember when we first came? Pickens wouldn't take his eyes from us in his store."

My father looked at her a moment, then smiled and pulled her arm through his. "Bess," he said. "It's time to go home."

My hands still had some tremble as I followed Momma and Papa down the boardwalk. To distract them, I picked up some tiny stones and tossed them one by one into the dust of the road. "Rose!" my mother said, and I had to stop.

We passed Rabbi Zeilonka, whose face looked solemn beneath his dark, wide-brimmed hat. Momma made a curtsy at him, and he put one finger along his nose and bowed to Papa. Rabbi Zeilonka is a dignified person of powerful words, but in size he is far from a giant. So am I, but to my surprise, when I passed him our shoulders were nearly level. Momma would soon be fussing again about needing to lower my hems.

Piano music was floating through the air as we approached the Brunckhorst Hotel. Tinkly and light as a birdcall, it was undoubtedly springing from the hands of Miss Polly. Her aunt Lucille is an enthusiastic player, but the effect she has on the piano is more barnyard poultry than sparrow of song.

I slowed my feet as we approached the hotel doors. Though I am a person of strictest honesty, Abe's dishonesties prevented me from telling Momma and Papa the true reason I had to stop there.

Luckily, I noticed one of my bootlaces had come undone, and I bent to fidget it. My parents walked on a way before noticing I wasn't behind them. Finally Papa turned and raised his hand, beckoning.

"I have a question for Miss Polly about the history assignment she gave on Friday," I told him. Now, this was strictly true. I had been gazing out the schoolhouse window at a man riding by on a horse when she gave the weekend reading pages—never mind that the assignment was always fifteen pages, and the previous night's was pages 53 to 68.

Momma's brow puckered like she was working up a lecture. "I'll be home in time to help with supper," I said. Papa nodded, and grabbed Momma's arm before she could spout a single word about The Dangers of Young Ladies of My Age Parading About Unescorted.

Chapter
3

I pushed open the twin oaken doors of the Brunckhorst Hotel and peered into the cool dimness.

"Rose?" a voice called. "You'd better come on in out of the heat."

Miss Polly wore the kind of starched white shirtwaists that looked prim and stuffy on everyone else, but made her look as bright as the moon in a winter sky. In the dusty piano corner in the lobby of the Brunckhorst Hotel, she fairly glowed.

She looked up from the piano keys and smiled. "I was hoping someone would show up to join in on 'Close to My Heart,'" she said, and made the piano trill something ripply and light.

As I sat next to her on the bench and watched her fingers fly, I felt a pinch of sadness that I was bringing bad tidings when she was in a mood to make such happy music. I let her play on a whole minute more than I could stand.

"Miss Polly," I said finally, "I have news."

"News?" Miss Polly said. Her playing slowed and then got quicker. "Well," she said, dropping her voice and glancing toward the other side of the lobby where some men in vests were ruining the air with cigars, "it must be important."

I paused a moment for the biggest effect, and then, in my lowest whisper, said, "I saw him."

Miss Polly's hands played stumbling music, like they'd forgotten what they were doing on the keys. "Him?" she said.

"His picture," I said. "In the newspaper."

The piano gave an ugly jangle, which caused some of the smoking men to peer at us through their smelly cloud. Miss Polly sat back on the bench, her face gone pale as her blouse.

And then I realized what my words had made her think.

"Oh no, not that!" I said. "Not in the funeral pages!"

I grabbed the sheet music and fanned it at her face, and then I just straight-out did it—gave her the whole terrible truth.

"Yes, Miss Polly," I said when I'd finished. "I'm sorry to say that I believe my brother lied to us. I'm sorry as well that I must tell you he appears to have become a low-living, lawless thief."

Miss Polly sat very still for a long, long moment, but then she lifted her hands and set them back on the keys. When she began to move them again, the music she made was a march. She plunked at the keyboard powerfully, shaking the piano with the force of the song. And then she started to hum.

I had to marvel a little at how calmly she was taking the news.

"How did he look?" she said at last, her eyes on a spot on the wallpaper.

"He appeared hairy," I replied. "Ragged as an old broom. He's gained a moustache and doesn't appear to have enjoyed much soap and water."

What I really wanted to tell her was that Abe's appearance was downright dreadful. But truth or not, I knew nobody wanted to hear their beloved looked like every last mule on the mule train had run over him, and then the wagon too.

"I'm sure he's not eating well," I said. Miss Polly responded with a pair of high, prancing chords.

"Oh, that's right," she said. "No cheese with his supper meat, or even milk. No risen bread or cake in early springtime, and no pig meat ever." She said it singsong, like she was repeating a rhyme for the first graders. Her voice was as smooth as the pleats on her shirt, and it did strike me again as odd that my great revelation hadn't stolen much of her peace.

"You're taking this well," I told her.

She played on awhile before saying, "Did Tough-as-the-Dickens Pickens recognize him too?"

"No," I said, without telling her the sticky-sweet reason why.

She smiled and tucked her head down toward the keys. "That brother of yours," she said. "I told him—" and she stopped abruptly, like people do when their mouth is about to let loose something they've decided it shouldn't.

Her hands had stopped too, but she made them work

again. "Try not to worry about Abraham, Rose," she said, turning to smile at me. "He'll be home eventually, safe and sound."

She sounded so certain. So calm.

So knowing.

And that's exactly what told me what her mouth would not.

She already knew about La Cucaracha.

She *knew*.

I used to carry around a painted wooden doll that had once been my mother's. It was hollow and cut in half, and if you twisted its top from its bottom, a smaller doll in its belly was revealed. In the smaller doll's belly was a doll even smaller, and so on and so on, until the last, which was just a tiny painted nub. It seemed to me now that my brother was also ordered in this way. Inside of Abe was a nested stack of secrets, but at their very center lay a lumpen, steaming lie.

Aunt Lucille came fluttering into the parlor. She was fresh from the kitchen, most likely, because her hands and apron were floury. Dora, her little brown dog, trailed after her. When Dora saw me, she wiped her wet nose on my stocking and made her tail wag fast. I'm not as fond of dogs as most dogs would wish, and this just seems to make them try harder to win me over.

"Rose!" Aunt Lucille said, beaming at me. "Did Polly spill the news?"

"Not yet," Miss Polly said.

"Well, I will, then," she replied, her smile spreading even wider. "We have made a plan to have ourselves an amusement next Saturday afternoon," she said, drawing her fingers through the curls dangling from the sides of her hair and leaving them streaked with flour. She squeezed her mouth tight like it was about to burst, and then her words pushed out in a breathy rush. "We shall perform for our guests selections from *The Mikado*, which is Mr. Gilbert and Mr. Sullivan's very latest musical, straight from London, England!"

"Now, Aunt Lucille," Miss Polly said, "that isn't strictly true."

"Well," Aunt Lucille said as she leaned toward the mirror glass next to the piano, "it may not be new to the world, but it is new to us." She didn't seem to notice the flour.

"We have the loveliest role for you, Rose," she continued, "a character of the name Pitti-Sing."

Miss Polly nodded. "It's the perfect part for your range," she said, "and it will be nice to share your talent with our guests." She bent over and picked up Dora, who stared at me from her shoulder with damp, pleading eyes.

I saw a newsreel once that featured a woman singing on a fancy stage in front of a roomful of people. She closed her eyes, like her singing came from a place she could only reach without using them. When she finished, the crowd applauded wildly and threw flowers at her feet. At that moment, every bit of me wished I was her. I wished it even though I full well knew it would never, could not ever, ever possibly come to pass.

"I can't," I said to Miss Polly. "I'm sorry."

Aunt Lucille turned away from the glass. "But we've

thought it all through," she said. "We will commence at four o'clock. It will be on Saturday, so there won't be church, and your mother will have no objections about schoolwork missed. You'll be home well before dark."

My father liked to joke about impossible things. "That will happen when pigs fly," he'd say, or "When a man walks on the moon." And even though I knew there was a greater likelihood of Rabbi Zeilonka riding a bleating sheep through the streets of El Paso than of my father agreeing to let me sing in front of a crowd of idle hotel guests, my heart made a little skip.

"Saturday," I said, "is our day for resting. And even if it wasn't, my father would tell me no."

"But…really, dear," Aunt Lucille said, casting an anxious glance at Miss Polly. "Your father didn't seem to have a problem allowing you to sing—which you did so prettily—at last year's end-of-school picnic. A lovely voice for singing is not a treasure all can claim, and surely there can be no harm in sharing it."

There was a reason Papa didn't mind my singing at the picnic, and it was because Miss Polly had simply turned to me after we'd eaten our sandwiches and asked me to. But how could I possibly explain my father's strict ways to Aunt Lucille? I looked down at the carpet and used my boot toe to trace its pattern of lush roses and tumbling buds.

"This will be a matter to ponder," Miss Polly said, and put a hand on her aunt's sleeve. "Anyway, you can practice with us now, Rose. Just for a minute or two."

"Well…," I said, glancing up to the pretty painted hall clock. It was ticking almost supper time. "Just for a minute."

Chapter 4.

The songs from *The Mikado* hummed in my head all the way home. The melodies made us press our voices down like springs, and then release them to sail up and up, higher than the flight of any soaring bird.

My mother's voice sought me as the front door clicked shut. "Rose! You are very late!" She came hastening toward me through the long hall, holding out a white apron like the one she was wearing.

"It is not only yourself you need to think about," she said, setting the apron on my middle and tying it tight. "Especially on such a night when we share our food!"

Papa hadn't mentioned guests, which meant guests had not been expected.

But that was not unusual. Our house was sometimes as busy as the Brunckhorst Hotel. Visitors arrived from lands across the ocean, from places named Vilna, Minsk, and Riga. They dressed oddly, and they smelled of the herbs they carried to keep off illness, of close quarters and worse.

They were gratefully polite to us, but with each other they were often given to shouting in their odd tongues.

My parents didn't seem to notice any of this. When the guests came, Papa brought out bottles of sweet, dark wine and talked with them late into the night. And as they sat together laughing and trading stories, my parents would glance at me and one would be sure to say, *Poor Rosala, only three years of age when we left Russia. She knows nothing but America,* as if this was my greatest loss. Eli had been ten and Abraham was eight, but it was only Abraham who would speak to me of things he remembered from our life there—the way Papa used to set me on the back of the big horse he used for plowing the field, the mean neighbor dog that once nipped hard at my hand, and the jumble of grandparents and cousins who lived all around us. He told me also of the freezing cold night when soldiers came to force Papa to serve once again in the czar's army, and the terrible things that followed when he told them he would not go.

Many of the guests who came to our house in El Paso had stories like that as well. Some stayed with us just long enough to find their own lodgings, but others lingered on and on and on. They remained long after I'd grown weary of sleeping on the stiff parlor sofa, of sharing and stretching every bite of food, of speaking nothing but the throaty, rough tongue of Yiddish, the only language I could use with them because very few knew English yet.

My mother is a woman whose temperament tends toward impatient, but she's entirely different when Papa brings home strangers. "Your father's heart is the size of the sun," she'll say as we peel buckets of potatoes or chop more cabbage to plump up the soup. I have even seen her wipe tears from her eyes as she said this, and without even a single slice of onion in sight.

The one thing I liked about hosting was when visitors brought daughters near to my age. Unlike most girls I knew in El Paso, they would speak with me of things beyond the styles of hair and clothing. I could take them to the dry creek bed to hunt for pretty stones. I could even show them my doll, a possession my mother scorned as childish the moment I turned the age of twelve.

"Are there children?" I asked as I took up the paring knife and settled in front of the carrots.

Momma flicked a potato eye into a bucket. "It is just one single man of twenty years." And then she raised her head and gave me her sweetest smile, the kind that made her cheeks rise high so her eyes closed nearly to slits. It was not a sight I'd expected to see, considering I'd made her angry with my lateness.

"We don't get so many of them, Rosie," she said. "Men so young and so unmarried. Why, he's merely seven years older than you are. You're a bit young to be thinking of these things, but not by much—your father is my age plus eight years. And I was, as you know, just fifteen when we wed."

She'd started talking this way last summer, which was also the time she'd started to fuss at me about my plaits and my boots. *A lady's hair is flowing. A lady's feet wear soft, pretty shoes.* She'd been nagging at me day and night. But

I'd gotten quite skillful at handling her when she was in the way of giving me a good pester. I took her words and made them into soft, pretty summer clouds sailing up over my head and into the endless acres of the sky. Sheep flocks, sky ships, wisps of cotton. They became sunset clouds this night, fluffy white, rippled with streaks of pink.

It was three days before the start of the holiday of Passover, and Momma decided this would be the night when we started our extra cooking. There were the jars of honey-sticky *haroses* to make and horseradish to grate, but most important, we had to start on the matzoh, the flat bread we'd eat for all eight days of the holiday. Matzoh baking wasn't a hard task. No time was spent waiting for it to rise—the dough is just patted flat and put into the oven to cook till it has gone crisp and hard.

It was certainly an easier chore than preparing the carrots. I had a deep scrape on one finger where I'd removed a piece of my own peel.

"Are you finished yet, Rosala?" Momma said with her finest honeyed voice. "It is time to serve our guest his tea."

◆

The young man had a dark red beard so thin it looked like it could have been dirt from his travels, and pale skin as soft as the palm of a baby's hand. The Texas sun would soon fix that—the strip of nose his hat didn't shade had already begun to turn the color of fire. His name was Shmuley, and he'd gotten off a ship three days before at the port of Galveston. He was dressed like all the newcomers were, in the heavily loomed black clothing of the old country. But at his neck was an odd flash of color: a bright blue-figured kerchief twisted into a low, lumpy knot.

He was from eastern Poland, he told us, where Momma lived as a child, and her voice rose in excitement as they spoke of places she remembered.

Shmuley was a good eater—the skinny ones always were. He was a good talker too, even through all his chewing and crunching. Fortunately, he also had a fair bit of English, though with his accent, it was sometimes hard to tell. "Such a fine town, this El Paso Texas," he said as he forked up three more blintzes. "I heard on the boat of the glorious synagogues, the pious rabbi. It is true there is even a kosher butcher?" He gulped down his mouthful and took a huge slurp of tea.

Momma looked proud. "So true is this," she said, "that you're in his house!"

She refilled his cup and handed me the empty teapot to refill. "My husband, Sol, is also," she said, "the cantor in the synagogue."

"Does he sing at his work, then?" Shmuley said as he wiped at his face with a napkin.

"He sings at all he does. The man's voice is a gift."

"Ah, *naches* for the meat," Shmuley said, "to hear the prayers sung as it is sliced!"

"Proud meat!" Momma giggled. "Such a sense of humor!" She covered her smile with one hand and waved me toward the kitchen with the other.

"There is something you may not have heard of our town," she said just before the kitchen door swung shut behind me. "We also have some very charming girls near to marrying age."

It was wise of my mother to wait until I was in the kitchen to speak these words. If she'd said them in front of me, I would have spit out my tea.

Chapter 5

Rabbi Zeilonka has said the reason we eat hard matzoh on Passover is that it was the only food the Hebrew people could take as they ran from that persecuting Egyptian pharaoh thousands of years ago, the one who used them as slaves. They suffered for their freedom, and to remember that suffering, on Passover we eat matzoh instead of bread. No cake, no cookies, no *challah*, no pastry. Just matzoh, only matzoh. Eight days we eat it, which is a whole, entire week and a nibble of the next one. After the third matzoh day, I'm ready to eat anything else. The shavings of pencils, or the bark off trees.

But if eating matzoh had some magical quality that could set me free from the persecutions of my mother, I would gladly chew it every day for rest of my life.

It took a long moment for Shmuley to reply to Momma's remark. "Your daughter seems delightful," he said at last. "But she cannot be more than the age of ten."

Momma made a huffing sound. "Why, she's thirteen last month. And already, such a wonderful cook! Her *kreplach* are light and fluffy, and the flavor of her brisket is unequaled."

"Thirteen," Shmuley said thoughtfully. And then he said the strangest thing. "Does she perhaps know of riding a horse?"

I took as long as I could with the tea, but eventually I had to come out of the kitchen. At the sight of me, Momma quit talking. Shmuley put down his cracker. And then he smiled, displaying a large empty window between his two most prominent teeth.

"Rosala," Momma said, offering her cup for refilling, "no more fussing in the kitchen. Come and sit. There's room there on the davenport," and she pointed to the spot on the sofa next to Shmuley.

I refilled his cup too, and sat down, pressing as close as I could to the arm of the sofa.

"And so, Mr. Schnitzler, why did you choose to emigrate to Texas instead of the Eastern states?" my mother asked. Her voice had suddenly gone low and proper.

"Ahhhh," he said, and his bony hand went up to his kerchief. "The Vild Vest!" Like most of the newcomers, Shmuley's W's were more like V's.

"I show you," he said, and dug in his coat pocket and pulled out a little book with worn, shaggy edges. There was a pair of galloping horses on the cover, ridden by two grim-looking young cowboys.

"I purchase in Hamburg," he said, "when there was delaying for the papers of emigration." His face flushed an even deeper red, and his eyes glistened. "And reading it poked at me, here"—he thumped a fist to his chest—"like an arrow from an Indian bow. And I thought, what great country is this America, where the women carry guns!"

It was a very odd statement, and what he did next was odder still. He caressed the cover of the book like it was a dog or a pet bird. Small wonder it was near to falling apart.

"And so," he continued, "I am here!" And with that, he laid the book down, pulled his blue kerchief over his nose, and stuck his hands in his pockets. And then he yanked them out, aiming his forefingers at Momma. "Bang bang!" he said, and he pulled the kerchief down and grinned at me again. I could just about see right down the back of his throat through that toothy little divide.

Momma seated me next to Shmuley at dinner. He was the only person I'd seen besides Abraham to eat nearly an entire roasted chicken. He kept lifting up his fork and waving it toward my mother, like a salute. My mother just waved her fork back, tines pointed at me, though the only part of the food preparation I'd had any hand in was the carrots. My father asked him some questions about the ship voyage, but mostly he just watched Shmuley eat.

After Papa finished his soup, he wiped his mouth on his napkin and turned to me.

"So, Rose," he said. "How was your visit at the hotel?"

His question took me by surprise, and as I worked up an answer, I could feel it all over again—the sweet, thrilling music, and the songs, light as bubbles of soap. I should have pinched my lips shut with my fingers, because these feelings seemed like they were about to spill right out of my mouth. And then they did.

"Papa," I said. My voice had a small tremble. "There's to be an amusement there next Saturday. It's a performance of an operetta called *The Mikado*, and Miss Polly and her Aunt Lucille say I'm just the perfect person to sing the part of—"

Papa held up his hand, slicing my sentence as cleanly as his big, gleaming butcher knives cut through a joint.

"Rose," he said. And then he just shook his head slowly. No, no, no.

"But Papa," I said. "It's just for a little while. We eat cold food on Saturdays, and I'll be home in plenty of time to help set out supper."

Momma put down her water glass and gave Papa a narrow-eyed glare. It was one of her darkest, most forceful looks.

"A promise to help in the kitchen," Papa said, "was made also today—a promise that was not, I think, well kept."

Momma nodded smugly, then gave a little start as though remembering she'd all but told Shmuley I'd cooked dinner single-handed. Luckily for her, the food seemed to be stuffing his ears as well as his mouth. He looked up briefly, but just to gesture at the carrots. Momma nodded at me, and I put a spoonful on his heaped-up plate. He took a bite and smiled.

Momma smiled back.

"My Rose peeled every one of them herself!" she said.

◆

It took a while for Shmuley's eating to finally stop, and when it did, Momma and I left him and Papa in the parlor and returned to the kitchen to resume the cooking of the Passover foods. Momma assigned me the making of the *haroses*, and though I generally find chopping nuts and apples tedious, on this night I was glad for the distance it would give me from Bang Bang Blue Kerchief.

But it didn't keep me from hearing about him.

"Of course he's too old for you now," Momma said as she patted dough into a circle. "But in three years he'll be just right. I admit, fifteen was young to marry, but sixteen will be perfect, and if you wait until nineteen, no one will want you. It's a wonderful match, Rose. He's very scholarly, and he has the boot-making trade."

I just kept cutting the apple bits without saying a word. "People always have need for new boots, don't they?" she persisted. Still I didn't answer.

My silence didn't suit her. By the time I was ready to mix the apples with honey, Momma looked fit to explode. She snatched the bowl from my hands, picked up the big spoon, and roiled the apples and nuts like they were laundry in a washtub.

"Rose Solomon," she said, huffing with her efforts, "I was blessed with two sons, not three. You can put boots on your feet, but it will not make you a boy. You can keep your hair in braids, but braids will not keep you a child. You will soon be a woman, and making a good match will be the most important thing you'll ever do. And the sooner you understand that, the better!"

It was harder this time, but I did it. Her words grew into clouds with high, round tops and flat, swift undersides. Glistening white, they were, with just the least purple hint of storm.

But Momma wasn't finished. "Tomorrow," she said, setting the bowl on the table with a thump, "you will comb out your hair and you will gather it at the back of your neck in a ribbon, like every other young lady your age has been doing for a year. You will wear the calfskin shoes you got for your birthday, and you will come straight home from school and work on stitchery!"

A pinch-footed, ribbon-bound prison. That's what Momma was plotting for my future. I tried, I really tried to conjure the clouds again, and I managed, but they were black and boiling with thunder. And before I could stop it, out came a blast of lightning.

At the very top of my voice I shouted, "WHY CAN'T YOU JUST LEAVE ME ALONE?"

Chapter 6

I felt quite horrible the instant those loud words left my lips. The look on Momma's face made me feel even worse. She clutched at a chair back like she was close to falling, and her mouth gaped and shut, gaped and shut. And then I heard my father's voice calling from the parlor. "Bess?" he said. "Something's come in the mail that I think you should see."

She pressed at the locket that lay over her heart, turned away from me, and *slap, creak, bang*, pushed open the kitchen door and whirled out of the room.

I grabbed up the broom and tried to sweep my hard words into the apple peels. I scrubbed at them on the table-top, washed at them with the sticky pots. But nothing could make them go away.

It was entirely Abraham's fault that the dark clouds split open. If he were home, he would have distracted Momma with an amusing story, or stepped between us with clever, soothing words. And then the clouds would have soared harmlessly off.

The oven timer trilled, which meant the matzoh was done. And what happened next was the most awful thing of that whole awful day. It was then I realized that for the first time ever, Abraham would not eat any of our matzoh. He would not enjoy the sweet *haroses*. He would not join us to dip the bitter herbs in salt water or drink the thick purple wine, because this Passover, Abraham would be far from our *seder*, or anyone else's.

My stomach went heavy, like it was full of rotted fruit.

God would let my brother know what he thought of his behavior. He'd occupy himself with coloring new birds when Abraham quarreled with his friends, the lawless outlaws. He'd be too busy counting grains of sand to intervene when Abraham and his murdering gang were finally caught. And he'd focus hard on managing a sunset when Black Jack Pershing finally cleaned out every single *bandido's* clock.

A cold, awful fear settled over me. The more I tried not to think of Abraham, the more I couldn't stop. I tried to picture him in a circle of golden light, wrapping it around him like a blanket of safety, spinning it over him like a cocoon. But no matter what I did to the image of Abe in my head, I couldn't keep the gold circle from quickly fading away.

◆

Momma never returned to the kitchen. When I finished wiping the last pot, I crept up the back stairway and got into bed. But sleep would not come to me. As I turned in the sheets, I heard the sounds of my parents' voices.

Papa's was low, but Momma's was pitched high. She

was doubtless complaining to Papa how coarse this coarse place had caused me to act, how rude my speaking had grown, how if I'd been raised in Russia, I would not be so ill-mannered. I got out of bed and crouched next to the wall to hear her words.

"I won't be able to sleep a wink. How can I, not knowing if my son is alive or dead?"

I drew a quick, sharp breath. Had they seen that photograph at Pickens's right through the molasses?

"Now, Bess," my father's voice said. "There's no reason to think Abraham has met with harm."

Her voice came again, thick with sobs. "But why would he tell us such a lie? That letter from your sister was very clear. He never arrived in Brooklyn."

My father's voice was soothing. "We've had his own letters," he said. "And Eli wrote to say he'd arrived. He even said Abraham was helping him sell fish from his pushcart."

Momma made a sound of disgust.

"Eli could have faked those letters from Abe—their writing is almost the same. Am I supposed to be comforted that my only responsible son would lie for his brother?" Momma's tone had gone from fearful to angry.

Papa gave a low chuckle. "It is not a curse to have two sons who care enough for us to hide what we might find troubling. Does it really surprise you that our youngest boy desired a different adventure than the one we wanted him to take?"

There was a long stretch of quiet before Momma spoke again. "Sol," she said. "I felt him today. It was as if he was with me, right there in Pickens's store. And the feeling he gave me was that there was trouble."

I heard Papa make a *tsk-tsk* noise. "Why do you fret so for Abraham? You did not do this when Eli left."

Momma gave a long sigh in return. "My Eli is our steady boy. He was never a worry. My Abe has never been anything but."

"Abe is fine, Bess," Papa said. "He's just fine in a different place than he told us he'd be, and tomorrow we'll send a telegraph to Eli and get the truth. You must stop fretting."

"I know that with my head," Momma said, "but my heart hasn't heard it. Abraham thinks the world is a feast, and he will not rest until he has tasted every part of it. But you and I know the world has flavors both bitter and sweet."

"Bess," my father said, "if a man is destined to drown, he can drown in even a spoonful of water."

My mother's response was a wail. "Drown!" she said. "There are oceans full of water near Brooklyn City, and for all we know, Abraham's in one of them!"

I heard the sound of a chair scraping and Momma's sob, followed by the scurry of Papa's feet across the floor. I knew what he was doing—fumbling for the bottle of her heart pills, pushing two of them into her mouth, tipping a sip of water in after them from the glass kept beside their bed. I held my breath as I listened, hoping the next thing I heard wouldn't be Papa running down the stairs and out the door to fetch the doctor.

Long minutes passed, and then finally Papa's voice came again. "Momma," he said, "our Abraham always finds his feet when he tumbles. He'll be just fine. And he'll show this world a thing or two. He will, Bess, you'll see."

◆

I was awake long after their voices stilled, and when I finally found sleep, it came with a terrible dream.

We were having the *seder*, but my mother's fancy ceremonial plate was horrifyingly wrong. The bitter herbs were cactus thorns, and the shank bone was dripping blood onto the carpet. There were two boiled eggs instead of one, and they rolled on the plate like they were tracking me. I looked out the window and my heart gave a hop, because there he was, my brother Abraham, riding a horse across a desert land. It was a fierce white creature that snorted steam from its mouth and bucked wildly, pitching Abe this way and that. They came to an enormous ditch, and when the horse leaped across it, Abe came off of the saddle. As he sailed through the air, he gave a long, heartbreaking wail. *Roooooose!*

By morning I knew what I had to do.

I got out of bed when the sky finally started to show color, and crept down to the kitchen, slowly, so the steps wouldn't make noise.

I lit the lamp, found writing paper and an envelope, and I wrote my brother a letter.

Dear Abraham,

I did not want to do this but you have left me no choice. Things have gone too far. Far farther than they should have. It has grown clear to me that you need to be saved from your own regretful impulses, and so I must insist you return home by Passover first night, which, if you have no calendar, is this Thursday. That is three days from this one. If you do not, I will tell Momma and Papa the Real Truth about where you've gone and I do mean every scrap of it. Every Scrap. And I may just add on about you and Miss Polly as well.

I know far more than you think I do.

Your loving sister,
Rose

I sealed the envelope tight and put Abe's name on it, and then I found a piece of Papa's heavy brown paper and wrote on it the truth—that I'd gotten up early because of a special errand. I put it on the kitchen table, blew out the lamp, and set off for Brunckhorst's.

I found Aunt Lucille in the kitchen. She was busy with the boarders' breakfast, but pointed me to Miss Polly, who was laying out plates in the dining room. My face must have showed my feelings, because Miss Polly took my hands and pulled me into the hallway. "Tell me quickly," she said. "Tell me what is wrong."

"I need to send a letter to Abraham," I told her. "He must get it as soon as can be."

Miss Polly is no-nonsense right down to her shoe buttons. "All right," she said without asking any more. "Silas Bridgewater's been transporting the letters you've given me for Abe. He's got a wagon route for peddling his vegetables. He doesn't disclose exactly how he gets our correspondence to Abe and his back to us, but he does, and that's all that matters. You're in luck—he doesn't usually leave until seven o'clock. You can find him at Kelsey's Livery, at the end of Montana Avenue."

There was a clatter from the kitchen, and then the sound of Aunt Lucille's voice.

"Hat pins and javelinas, Polly! If I'd wanted to ruin myself with hard work, I'd have married that one-armed wheelwright!"

"I'm so very sorry I can't go with you," Miss Polly said, turning toward the kitchen, "but we've got a land-office crowd in here today. Silas is a fine and decent fellow—his son Thurman was a boarded student here, and first in class. You can trust Silas with your note."

She turned back to the hall and went quickly to the little desk behind the door. She wrote something on a piece of pink-colored paper, folded it into a pink envelope, and then turned away from me to try to hide the little kiss she placed on it. "Give him this as well," she said, and she smiled a shy smile.

There came another crash came from the kitchen. Aunt Lucille let loose with more spicy talk and a scream.

"Oh dear," Miss Polly said as she hurried across the dining room. She paused at the kitchen door. "One thing, Rose," she said. "Try not to speak to anyone, and hurry right back. You promise?"

I nodded, and she was gone.

Chapter 7

I'd been to Kelsey's Livery before, but always with Papa. It was situated on the very edge of town, near the wide desert that stretched beyond El Paso. The desert was a vast and terrifying place, and Momma and Papa had forbidden me to venture there. But every step was taking me closer to it.

I felt odd tingles rustle up and down my shoulders, like the brush of feathers. It might have been the feeling of excitement, but I was too scared to tell.

The board sidewalk ended, and I had to walk in the dust-thick roadway. The streets grew narrower, and the buildings turned faded and rough. My friend Anna Rooney told me that this part of town housed "roughneck drunks" and "ladies who weren't ladies." I didn't know what she meant by that, and was wishing I'd pressed her for more information. Lately she'd taken to laughing at my questions and telling me I was a simple child who didn't know the ways of the world. Lately I could only get along with Anna by pretending everything she told me was something I already knew.

I passed few people as I walked, and it seemed they all looked at me curiously. I tried to make my feet step hard like they knew what they were doing, and pulled my bonnet up over my head to let me hide in its shade. Not a soul watching me would have known how I really felt.

Finally I reached a wooden corral with horses in it, and a low barn building with KELSEY'S LIVERY lettered across the side of it in peeling green paint. There were two motorcars out in front, and an old, beat-up hoop-top wagon. A sandy-haired boy stood before it, adjusting the harness of a large brown horse.

I stood a moment behind the horse, wondering what to do next. When the boy spoke, it made me jump.

"You, there," he said. "Old Rogers kicks, so you shouldn't stand behind him. But I warn you—he bites as well."

His voice was stern, but he had a wide, cheerful face, topped with hair that flopped over one eye like a stray dog's.

"I'm looking for Silas Bridgewater," I said, in a louder voice than I'd meant to.

"Rogers," he replied, turning to the horse and stroking its mealy-colored nose, "the little girl has the voice of a young lady."

I was glad my bonnet hid my flush.

"I'm Thurman Bridgewater," he said.

"My name is Rose Solomon," I said. "Miss Polly Brunckhorst sent me."

The boy came around to my side of the horse and peered at me quite directly. And then he said, "And am I then addressing the very Miss Rose who is the sister of Abraham Solomon?"

I was so flustered I couldn't do more than nod, but Thurman kept talking, so it didn't matter.

"I hope you know," he said, "what a truly great cause your brother is aiding. Truly, truly great. If my Pa didn't need my work…"

I had no idea what he was speaking of, and was starting to tell him so when Thurman raised his hand to shush me and turned his head to the left. And then I heard it too: a muffled clop of hooves, and the low rasp of men's voices.

It was Thurman's turn to look nervous. "Here," he said. "Step into the wagon a minute, if you'd be so kind."

"I have school—" I said, but he put a hand on my arm.

"Just until they pass," he said, and pushed me firmly toward the flap of the canvas.

Chapter 8

The wagon smelled of spoiled cabbage and mold. There was a pile of blankets inside, and a heap of some sort of goods covered by cloth. When I brushed against them, they shifted with a clink.

The hooves stopped close by.

"Good day to you, boy," one of the men said. "Mind saying what's in your wagon?"

"I'm taking a load of catawbas to Salt Flat," Thurman replied. He said it in a voice that suddenly seemed to be squeezing through a smaller pipe.

"Just catawba melons?" the man said, in a way that showed he needed some convincing. "Someone around here's been trading firearms with the Villistas. You hear anything about that?"

"I don't know much of town affairs," Thurman said. "Pa and I trade here, but we farm up in Bandolero. Haven't seen no guns around, save Pa's Smith & Wesson. I'm not carrying it today, though. Pa took it shooting rabbits."

I shifted, and the lumpy pile next to me clinked again.

"Rabbit shooting," one of the men said. "You hicks eat anything." The other man laughed, and I smelled the sharp odor of a lit match and then a strong whisper of tobacco.

"Not that a green boy like you'd be trading guns with those bloody Mexicans," the man said. "I heard that Villa feller would just as soon kill a person as look at them. But not before he had a little fun first. Bind you to a cactus and cut it open to bring the ants, like that farmer in Frontera. Or force you to dig your own grave and stand in it when they shoot you."

There was nothing at all amusing in this tale, but for some reason all of them laughed, even Thurman, though his sounded false. The man said another thing—I couldn't hear exactly, but it sounded like "Spit in your eye and charge you for an eyewash," and everyone laughed again. Then there came the sound of clinking glass, and a faint, awful whiff of drinking liquor. The men grew louder, and their talk more foolish. Finally there was a creak of saddle leather, and at long last the shuffle of hooves.

I waited a quiet minute, then crawled toward the canvas flap and pushed it aside. Thurman startled when he saw me. His face had gone very serious.

"You, girl," he said. "You need to get home to your mother."

"I have a letter," I said. "It must—" but Thurman held up a hand to stop me. There were more voices in the alley now, and he took hold of my arm and pushed me back into the wagon. He reached into his coat pocket and took out some-thing that gave a sharp-edged glint in the dim light. But then he put it back in.

"Here," he said. "I've got to pull inside." He jumped onto the wagon seat and chirruped to the horse. I fell back against a wooden rib as the wagon gave a jerk and rolled into the dark hole of the stable.

I heard the thud of Thurman hopping down onto the dirt. And then he gave a small puff of breath, the kind you make when you're halfway to sitting and notice a lizard on your chair. I crawled to the front of the wagon bed and peered out between the flaps. A man was holding Rogers's reins. He was a thick-waisted, dark-tanned fellow, wearing clothes creased with dirt, and even in the barn shade his eyes looked sun-squinty. When he spoke, he had the accent of the Mexican folk.

"*Hola!*" he said. "*Amigo*, you are looking for someone, are you not?" His voice was low, but something about the way it sounded just about stopped my breath.

"I'm only a farmer, sir, here to trade a load of melons for some laying hens," Thurman said, but the words came out so choked, it made me think his breath was in the same bad way.

The man laughed. "Oh ho, the chief will like that. We are much in need of melons." He reached into his pocket and pulled out a small bag. He poked it with his forefinger and it gave a little jingle. "And we've got all the chickens you need, no, my friend?"

He didn't say "friend" in any kind of amiable way. And I couldn't help wonder who else was lurking nearby to allow him the claim of "we."

Thurman's mouth made a strung-tight smile. "All right," he said, trying a more confident note that nearly convinced. "Where shall I unload?"

The man smiled back without a drop of humor. "Move the wagon into the back, and we will talk more," he said.

Thurman guided the horse into the shadows. He turned Rogers so his head faced the doors, and whispered, "Under the blanket!" as he came near the front flaps. I'd had just enough time to cover myself when he stepped to the wagon's rear and pulled the back flaps wide. Through the width of a generous fray hole, I saw him yank the covering off his cargo and reveal a pile of shiny brown rifles.

And then I saw the shadows behind him move, and out of them stepped another man. This one was a tall fellow, with a ripped red flannel shirt and braces straining to hold his trousers against the press of his belly.

Thurman stacked the guns in the dirt, and the men began to count them. They counted to forty-five, which made the bigger one shake his head. "It was to be fifty," he said.

"The amount is what my father promised," Thurman said.

"The old man don't usually send fuzz-chin boys to do his work," the man said. His face was even uglier than the first man's. Dirtier, too.

"My father is ill," Thurman said. His father was sick at home to these men, rabbit hunting to the others. He certainly couldn't be doing both. Miss Polly had said Thurman was smart, but hadn't added anything about being truthful.

"You give him this medicine to help him get well," the less ugly man said, and he threw the bag of coins into the dirt. Thurman fetched it up and proceeded to count the money into his trouser pocket. And then he counted the coins from his pocket back into the bag, and then once more back into his pocket.

"Thirty-five a firearm was the price my father told me," he said, looking up at last.

"We've had to cut some out of that, seeing you kept us waiting so long in here with the flies and the stink."

"Yeah," the other one said. "We was inconvenienced." He gave a mean chuckle, and I followed his gaze to some wooden planks stacked against the wall. There was a man lying in the dirt next to them. He had a cloth tied over his eyes and another over his mouth, and he wasn't moving at all. "So we had to do something about it," Uglier said. The tied-up man gave a low moan. "And when Kelsey comes to, he won't let us meet here no more."

Chapter 9

As Thurman listened to Uglier's words, his face looked to be hosting a mighty struggle. "But what my father told me...," he said. "My father—" His voice cut out, and I leaned out farther to see why. Uglier had picked up one of the rifles and leveled it on his shoulder, the blasting end pointed at Thurman's nose.

"You'll have to explain to him how things worked out," he said.

Thurman's neck had gone red.

"The gun isn't loaded," he said. "You're just trying to bully me. It's ungentlemanly to back out on an agreement."

I had to press my hand to my mouth at Thurman's words. Mentioning gentlemanly behavior, at a time like this!

Less Ugly's right hand went into his trouser pocket. It came out with a very small gun. "The only agreements that bind are made from steel and gunpowder," he said, but he said it so calm and quiet, you'd have thought he was discussing whether it was noon or twelve o'clock.

I saw Thurman's hand groping toward the pocket of his coat. I clutched at the hoop-top canvas, and the words *"Thurman, no!"* flew right out of my mouth.

They burst with such force that the Uglies would surely have heard me if there hadn't at that very moment come a ground-shaking bang from the deepest part of the shadows. It was followed by a cloud of white dust that drifted quickly upward through the livery's few ribbony bits of light.

I reached out and yanked at Thurman's arm. He jumped into the wagon as Less Ugly yelled something loud and angry in the Mexican language. A shout came from the depths of the cloud, and then, after a moment, someone emerged from the dust.

Chapter 10

He was a short, slight fellow and he was covered in some kind of powdery substance, from the top of his head to the tips of his boots. He pulled off his neckerchief and ragged it across his face.

"*Perdón*," he said. "I was lifting the cornmeal barrel and *poof*! Slipped right from my hands." His voice was rough, but pitched high.

Uglier shook his head. "It is good for you that *El General* likes you and your people, friend," he said. "But the day he stops will be a very good day for—"

He didn't finish. Thurman had taken advantage of Uglier's distraction and crept to the wagon seat, where he grabbed the reins and cracked them against Rogers's fleshy back parts. He must have cracked them with all his might, because Rogers made a mighty leap toward the patch of sunlight that marked the doorway.

I wish Thurman had given some hint of his plan, a wink

or a whispered word, but no. And when the wagon jolted forward, it propelled me right out the back of it.

There was pain, noise, shouting. I landed hard on my hind end, and stayed there, trying to find my breath.

"*Pare!*" Less Ugly shouted. "*Stop!*" He ran after the wagon. "Watch her!" Uglier said, and ran out too. The cornmeal-dusted little man took hold of my hand and pulled me to my feet. "You picked yourself quite a place to play hide-and-seek," he said. His hands felt rough and callused.

From out in the street came the sound of running feet and shouting.

The man took hold of my arm and dragged me to the square of sunlight that marked the stable door. "You must go," he said.

The shouting was coming closer. "Go *now*," he said. "RUN!"

That was all the invitation I needed. I picked up my skirts and I flew down the street like the mud golem of Prague was chasing me.

Chapter 11

At the end of the block, I set a foot into a clump of horse refuse and had to do a quick-stepping dance to dislodge it. That was when I felt a sharp jerk on the back of my dress.

"*Señorita*," Less Ugly said, "why do you leave in such haste?" The grip he gave my arm was a painful one.

The man who had released me was standing out in front of the stable. As we approached, he folded his arms and shook his head.

"Nice job watching her, Al," Less Ugly said with disgust.

"We have no need to hang on to this child," the man named Al said. "We're gonna let her go." In the sunlight I could see that his face was smooth in contrast to the stubbled chins of his companions. I hoped that meant he was less rough inside as well.

"The Revolution cannot leave a trail of tattling tongues," Less Ugly said. "Why was she here, if not for spying?"

Al pulled his bones to his full height. "She's a little girl," he said. "We'll tell her we'll shoot her dog if she talks about this to anyone, and that will be that."

"No," said another voice. Uglier had returned too, alone. Thurman had apparently made a fine, fast getaway. Uglier spit on the ground and said something in Mexican.

Al's brow furrowed. "To cut a mountain trail you must do it alone?" he said.

Uglier threw his hands into the air. And then he leaned close to Al, but put his eyes on mine and said in painfully plain English, "To hide in plain sight works only if no one sees you. We take her to camp and let the chief decide."

I saw a twitch in Al's jaw. "*General* doesn't need this bother."

"We will let him tell us that," Uglier said, and he spit on the ground again.

I saw Al's hand move toward the pistol strapped to his waist, at the same instant Less Ugly reached into the pocket that held his little gun.

I once watched a newsreel that showed a war somewhere in the world. The men were shooting at each other with big guns, and some of them weren't very good at dodging bullets. It was a sight so awful I had to pull my bonnet over my eyes, and now, unless I stopped it, the very same thing was about to unfold right in front of me.

I had to act quickly.

"I wasn't spying," I said. "I was in Thurman's wagon by accident. I don't even know the fellow. I promise I won't tell anyone anything I saw or heard."

Uglier's face looked even worse when he smiled. "Oh

yes," he said. "So Thurman's *horse* must have told you his master's name." And he pulled out his gun and pointed its nose at Al.

My truth had just shoveled a deep ditch, then run behind me and pushed me in it. *They make you dig your own grave.* My head started spinning. My eyes went blurry. I needed to wipe my nose.

"Let's say we take her," Al said, loudly.

"Ah," Uglier said. "Now you talk like a revolutionary."

"But see, we can't do it," Al said. "We have only three horses, and the pack mules are loaded down with the rifles."

Less Ugly scratched at his whiskery chin.

"Well then," he said, "she rides with you."

◆

Al led me back into a corner of the barn. Horses were tethered there, and as he untied the reins to a large, bony white one, he muttered something in Mexican. It was most probably some kind of cursing.

Uglier rode up on a little brown horse and handed him a black bandanna.

"Over her eyes," he said.

Al was a bit rough with the knotting, but was decent enough to say "Sorry," and add, "It's better you don't see the route." He boosted me onto the horse's back and got onto the saddle in front of me.

"Well, girl," he said, "I did tell you to run."

"Yes," I said, hoping the next thing he said wouldn't be "Guess I should have told you to run *fast*."

"Agustino's not one for reasoning, and he's very quick to his pistol. But Villa's an evenhanded fellow. He'll probably just send you back home, and in the meantime you'll have a nice ride through the desert."

A nice ride through the *desert*? Was he making a joke?

"You ever been on a horse?" Al said.

There were Abe's stories of sitting me on Papa's plow horse in Russia, but I was too young to remember it. "No," I replied.

"In that case, hang on tight," he said, and made the horse spin around. "Giddyap," he told it. The horse's sides jiggled, like Al was nudging it with his boots.

But it didn't move.

I heard a sharp jangle like Al had poked at it with spurs. The horse didn't appear to feel it. The creature was either standing dead, or doing a first-rate imitation.

"Dang-blasted nag!" Al said.

I heard a mutter of disgust from one of the Uglies, and the sound of a loud smack. The horse shuddered, and then, quicker than you could say one-two-three, it went from expired to flat-out gallop.

I clutched at Al's shirt, his belt, the leather of the saddle. When the horse finally slowed, it settled into a gait that made me feel like I was riding the arm of Momma's treadle sewing machine. "I would tell you Blanca is a little stubborn," Al said as the horse jolted us along, "but that would be like informing you that rain is wet."

The soft sounds of the horse's hooves told me we'd stepped off the hard-packed city streets. The heavy press of sun heat on my neck told me we were heading right into the desert.

I was being kidnapped into the wilderness. I was being kidnapped by a band of desperadoes and thieves. I was being kidnapped to an unknown fate.

But Abraham would be there, I told myself, wherever *there* turned out to be. And he'd be plenty mad at his fellow villains for kidnapping me, too. Whatever foolishness he had gotten himself up to, he was still my brother. And he'd do all he could to make everything right.

In the meantime, the horse was disturbing my balance awfully. I had to strain with every muscle to keep from getting joggled right off. And as one mile bounced into the next, I started to wonder if I'd even be able to stay on long enough to face that hard-eyed man from the newspaper photograph, or if I would just meet my end under the feet of a cranky old horse.

Chapter **12.**

There was only one thing I knew about the creatures that lived in the desert, and it was that they were poisonous, painful, or both together. My friend Anna Rooney liked to list them for me in sinister detail: the snakes, the lizards, the scorpions. Apparently each one caused death in horrible, disfiguring ways. And if you by chance survived them, the coyotes, owls, and wild pigs would swoop in to finish you off.

I heard a rustling sound coming from down near the horse's feet. It was the snakes, most likely, squirming by the dozen right across the ground. Because of that blindfold, I wouldn't even get to see my doom before it hauled me off.

At long last Blanca left off the shaking gait and moved into a walk so ponderous she seemed to be crawling. And then she stopped altogether and grunted. There was a thudding sound, and the high, foul odor of elimination. I kicked at Blanca myself to move us quickly from it, and Al said something sharp to her.

"I know just a few words of the Mexican language," I said, hoping some talking would steer my thoughts from the murderous desert animals.

Al made a reply, but his tone was a harsh one. "The people are Mexican, and the language they speak is Spanish," he said. "Calling their language Mexican is a sign of both disrespect and ignorance." It was Anna Rooney who had taught me that term, and I'd seen Gabriela frown when she used it. So Al was probably right.

It seemed a good idea to wait a bit before talking again, so I counted hoofbeats to distract me.

I nearly made it to sixty-five.

"Where are you taking me?" I asked him.

"It's a very secret place," he replied.

"What kind of secret place?" I said.

"The less you know, the better," he said, "but there's no harm in telling that many people have found safety there."

"What kinds of people?" I asked.

"Every kind."

"Including Indians?" I said.

"Yes," he said, and clammed up once more.

In the silence that followed, there came a sudden strange image in my head of Shmuley, and the greatness of his gap-tooth pleasure if he were, at that moment, in my boots. Too bad we couldn't change places. And somehow that thought sent my thinking off to Thurman, who would have already gotten away if he were me. He was smart enough to carry a knife. The only weapon I had in my pocket was my letter.

Blanca felt like she was walking so slowly she was nearly going backward. One of the Uglies shouted something, and his voice was far enough away to be blurry. Al shouted something back, and I felt Blanca's sides quake with his kicking. Again, his spurs didn't impress her.

The blindfold was beginning to scour the skin from my cheeks. It hurt near enough to bring tears. "Can I please, please, take this thing off my eyes?" I said.

Al took a long time to answer, but finally he said, "All right. They've pulled far enough ahead." I felt the bandanna being tugged away, and then the sun on my face, which was blinding after the darkness of the cloth. I could hardly see a thing.

"I imagine you have a few questions," Al said. "About who we are. And why you're coming with us."

"I already know," I said. "You're Pancho Villa's men. In other words, a group of low-living thieves."

"Now, wait a minute," Al said. "We're not low-living thieves, and I'm not—" But I didn't let him finish.

"You're kidnapping me, that's obvious. And if you're taking me to the place where the rest of the Pancho Villa men are gathered, you'll face the wrath of my brother, who won't favor seeing his only sister mistreated."

"Your *what*?" Al said.

My bold words seemed to blaze me a path for even bolder ones.

"Yes. My brother Abraham Solomon is among your number. But I've got something right here that will cause there to be one less Pancho Villa bandit at your camp." And I pulled the letter out of my pocket and waved it for Al to see.

"As you all have probably learned by now, my brother has a terrible temper," I said. "Just you wait till he reads *this*."

"Abraham Solomon?" Al said.

"That's his name," I replied.

"Abraham Solomon," Al said again.

"Yes!" I said.

"There is no such person in Pancho Villa's army," Al said.

I felt my insides give a quiver, and for a second my mouth seemed unable to make proper words. "But he...he was in the paper. In a picture! Right next to the man himself!" I finally managed.

There came then the sound of Ugly's voice from much closer, and Al jerked the bandanna back over my eyes. Once again I was bumping along in darkness, and now, with shock and terror as company. Where could my brother be, if not in Pancho Villa's camp? And if he was not there, what would happen to me?

Finally Blanca's walk got jerkier, and her hoofbeats made a ringing sound. When the Uglies spoke to each other, their voices had an echo. Al called something to them, and then, with a jolt, Blanca stopped moving.

Suddenly the blindfold was pushed to the top of my head. I could see walls made of rock all around us, reddish in color, and pocketed with odd-shaped holes. We were in the middle of a canyon. The Uglies were nowhere in sight. Al chirped to Blanca and her hooves echoed loudly as she picked up her pace.

She felt different, like she was moving willingly at last. She gave a loud horse call and I heard it answered from somewhere up ahead. We climbed a steep slope and then moved down, into a narrow slot in the rock. It was dark in there, and the cliff came so close it scraped at my legs. Anna Rooney said scorpions liked dark the best.

I smelled fire smoke and saw light up ahead. Blanca stopped again and Al yanked the blindfold back down.

A hiding hole was where we were going, a place where no one would find me even if they came looking. The thought made me feel like I'd eaten uncooked bread.

The bandanna had loosened with moving, and it slipped a little on my left eye. I got a glimpse of rows of tents, some with men in front of them, a small herd of donkeys and goats, and clothes swinging from lines. I heard the voices of women and a sound of trickling water, and then wild barking and growling—the noise of dogs giving us chase. Finally Blanca stopped again. It must have been Al's idea, because he didn't try to make her go. I felt hands grasp my waist and then I was standing on the ground.

"There are some things you must know," Al said. "This is a rough place for a girl to be. Say as little as you can to anyone, especially him, because truth isn't always your friend here."

He pulled my bandanna off and tossed it into the dirt.

"And there is one more thing," he said.

But then his mouth snapped shut, and he turned back to the horse. "Never mind," he said.

Chapter 13

We were standing in the shadow of a huge cloth tent set apart from long rows of smaller tents. As Al led the horse to a water bucket, the sound of gunfire split the air. It was terribly loud, and terribly close, and it was followed by an angry shout.

Al did not seem disturbed by the noise. He just stepped near to the tent and called out, "*Hola!*"

The word was echoed by someone within. The wall flapped open, and a man with a large drooping mustache appeared in the hole. He said something else in his language, which was properly and respectfully called Spanish, and Al gave me a push, and we followed him inside. The place was dark as the inside of a medicine bottle, and there was a smell of gunpowder and tobacco smoke and rotten meat.

When my eyes adjusted to the dimness, the first thing I noticed was a fancy desk. It was made of some kind of yellow wood, and had wild faces carved on the corners and huge wooden feet with claws. There was a grand chair behind it, tall, with turned spindles, fit for a king.

Beyond it, on the farthest side of the tent, three men holding guns were staring at a table. One of them turned toward us and held up a hand like a warning. And then I saw what they were looking at: it was a large brown rat halfway up one leg of the table. There was a chunk of meat pegged on the wall, which was what the rat seemed to be heading for. When the creature's leg touched the top of the table, it let loose an awful squeal and jumped high into the air. The man in the middle raised his gun and blasted away, and the rat thudded to the dirt.

"Well done, *General!*" one of the men said. "Straight through the eye!"

The shooting man got up and walked toward the desk. As he came closer, I felt a shiver streak right down my back.

The shooting man was none other than that bandit, the notorious Pancho Villa, otherwise known as La Cucaracha, otherwise, *otherwise*, the man who had ruined my brother.

He was round in the face, with wild, dark hair. He wasn't overly tall or terribly handsome, but somehow when he sat down in that fine chair he did it with the air of a king.

"Al!" he said. "Did you see? We put metal on the top of the table, and hooked a wire from it to the battery of the motorcar. How they jump when they touch it!"

"Well shot, *General,*" Al said, and he strode forward and gripped Pancho Villa's hand. I heard a click and a squeak of leather. The other men were training their guns on Al.

"*Está bien, mis amigos,*" Pancho Villa said. He turned

back to Al and smiled. His teeth were mostly hidden by his thick moustache, but the few that weren't had the color of the desert earth.

"So," he said. *"Mi Blancita.* She gave you quite a ride, yes?"

Al nodded. "She's a fine, fine horse," he said. "I am very grateful for your generous offer to take her to town."

Pancho Villa chuckled. "But you found her a little spirited, not quite a lady's mount?"

Al smiled. "A mind of her own, you could say."

"You should see when she heads to battle! Like a wild animal, she is. She was not too much for you to handle?" Pancho Villa said, tilting back in his chair.

"No problem at all, Chief," Al said. Pancho Villa looked pleased.

I couldn't believe my ears. It was as if a pile of manure had been heaped between them and they were taking turns shoveling it back and forth.

The shoveling continued. "Many times she's tried to best me," Villa said, "grabbing the bit in her teeth and galloping swiftly as a storm wind."

"You're an expert, *General,*" said the man standing to the right of the desk.

"You could tame the mule deer and the buffalo," said the man to the left.

Pancho Villa acted like he hadn't heard them.

"And yet she allowed you to use her for a humble errand, in service of the Revolution," he said. "As I have seen again and again, the simplest horse is nobler than the wisest man."

My thoughts escaped my nose with a snort, and the sound drew his boiled eyes.

"Al," he said, "who is this girl?"

"We picked her up in El Paso," Al said. "She says she's an orphan who came out to stay with relatives, but they'd moved on. So she got herself a situation at the hotel, and she's working as a chambermaid until she earns stagecoach fare to catch up with them." As fluidly as a stream of water is the way this falsehood slipped from Al's mouth. I turned to look at him, but he didn't meet my gaze.

Villa frowned and shook his head. "Why was this child brought here?" he said.

I heard a movement behind me, and a slice of sunlight flashed into the tent. And then Less Ugly was standing next to us.

"*Jefe*," he said, "she is a spy. She saw the guns in the livery."

Al took a step forward. "She says she was in the livery looking for extra work. So she saw the guns. Who will she tell? And who would believe her?"

"She talks to you, eh?" Pancho Villa said, eyeing me. "She does not look talky."

Al nudged my boot with his own. "Why, that girl's got tongue enough for ten rows of teeth. Once she started to move her mouth, she slowed only to pull in breath." His lies were not streams of water. They were streams of spit.

Pancho Villa turned to me and beckoned. "Come here," he said. My legs took me to him quite slowly. Up close his eyes were gold-brown, not deep black as they'd looked in the picture.

"Girl," he said, "do you know who I am?"

Was I supposed to know him? Was I not? I turned my gaze to the floor.

Pancho Villa gave a snort. "You will hear some call me Chief, or *Jefe*, or *El General*. You will hear others call me Señor Villa. The people call me Pancho, but my mother, she named me something else. Thank God she is dead and cannot hear me called La Cucaracha. You know what that means?"

Was I supposed to know this? Was I not? I shook my head and ventured to look up. He smoothed his moustache and smiled. "It is the insect that crawls in filth."

"The cockroach," Al said, turning to me.

"So I should be insulted, no?" Villa said. I think I was supposed to shake my head again, but he didn't give me the chance.

"Well, I am not! *La cucaracha*, the cockroach, is quick-footed and daring. The cockroach stops at nothing to get what it wants. They try to squash me and they cannot. They try to trap me and I escape them!"

He reached into the top drawer of the desk and pulled out a long cigar. The man to his right struck a match to it.

"So you don't know me, little girl? To you, I am just a crazy man in the desert, eh? *This*, I think, insults me. Do your people not see the newsreels or follow the newspaper? I have been much in the papers. Does your father never read them?"

He leaned toward me, tobacco smoke leaking from his mouth, and suddenly my eyes were gathering water. My father. My mother would be hysterical when she discovered I was gone, but Papa's heart would crack into pieces. I tried to contain my tears, but they spilled from one eye and then the other. Soon, my face was covered in wet.

Pancho Villa dropped the cigar onto the desk, on a spot covered with burns. "*Dios mío*, an orphan, yes? Al says this, but I did not truly hear."

He fumbled in the drawer again, and held out a handkerchief.

"Please," he said.

And then the strangest thing happened. The tent flaps parted and the interior was flashed with a slice of light again, and in the center of it stood a beautiful little girl. She was wearing a frilly, flouncy dress in buttercup yellow, with a bonnet that matched it hanging by ribbons down her back. Her hair was black and shiny as the eye of a crow, done in plaits pinned all around her head, and she was altogether the prettiest thing, with red, red lips and bright brown eyes.

A sudden image of Anna Rooney came into my head. I could see her face as plain as if she was standing in front of me. The image spoke, and the words it said were *In a filthy hole like this, how could she ever manage to keep such a nice dress clean?*

Chapter 14

The girl walked toward us with an odd, lurching gait. I saw Pancho Villa's eyes glow with pleasure at the sight of her, but his mouth frowned sternly down.

Al was frowning too. "We've taken too much of your time, *General*," he said, and pulled me toward the tent flap.

"You are an American!" the little girl said, and she smiled, showing deep dimples. Her low, raspy voice didn't match the rest of her. "I heard you talk! I talk English too."

"*¿Qué occure, Dorotea?*" Villa said.

She limped to him and took his hand.

"Felipe says I must not ride Adelita for a while. But I *want* to ride Adelita."

Villa said something in Spanish to the man on his right. The man went through the flap of the tent and soon returned with another man.

This one wore a faded red blanket folded across his chest, and had a long, sorrowful face. His hair stuck tight to his head from sweat, and his hands pinched the brim of his wide hat as he unspooled what seemed like some kind of long, sad tale.

Villa turned to Dorotea and started to speak, but Dorotea wagged her finger at him. "*En inglés*," she said.

Villa sighed. "You hear what Felipe tells me. Adelita is lame. He thinks a stone has bruised the sole of her foot, and she needs rest to get better."

Dorotea's pretty smile slipped into a deep, sulky pout. "He said this to me already. But *Tío*, I'm just a little thing and Adelita is big. I will not hurt her."

She reached up and took hold of Villa's hand with hers. He squeezed it, then leaned toward her and brushed a wisp of hair from her face.

"Felipe is right," he said. "Adelita should rest. You can ride her soon, and for now you must ride another horse."

Dorotea pulled her hand away and shook her head so wildly, her plaits nearly sprang free.

"No!" she said. "It isn't true you must rest if you are lame. I am lame and do I not walk?" She pulled back the hem of her dress and displayed a terrible looking cage that captured her right leg from ankle to knee.

Pancho Villa's eyes went soft and drooping. "All right, *mi niña bonita*," he said, "all right." He turned to Felipe and spoke to him.

When Felipe replied something that sounded like a protest, Villa's eyes blazed with a sudden fierce fire. Felipe scurried out of the tent.

He turned back to the little girl.

"And that is all?" he said, trying to sound gruff.

"It is not," she said, as I knew somehow she would.

"I need someone to play with. Not Felipe. He tells me nothing but no, no, and no. And not Juanita. She dislikes Catalina, and is cross when I win at cards."

She looked right at me. She showed her dimples again. "What's her name?" she said.

Al put his fingers on my shoulder firmly, almost a pinch.

"We had just agreed, sir, had we not? The girl goes back. She's of no use to us, and she'd drive us all *loco* with her chatter."

"She likes to talk?" Dorotea said. "I like to talk too! There has been no one here to talk with since Inez and her daughter left. I like this girl's strange hair. I like her rough shoes. Does she play cards?" She directed none of this to me, like I was not a person with feelings, but a dog or a chair.

Al's fingers pressed harder on my shoulder.

"Oh please, oh please!" Dorotea said. She clasped her hands on the front of her dress and turned her eyes sad and begging. "*General*," she said, when Villa didn't respond. "Can't I have her?"

Pancho Villa leaned back once more in his royal chair. His cigar still smoldered on the desk, but he pulled another from the drawer. The man to his left tried to light it for him, but he waved him away and lit it himself. And then he sat without smoking, tugging at his brushy moustache. The cigar had gained a long tail of ash by the time he spoke.

"No family of her own, you said?"

"But she does have work," Al said, "Someone will notice if she doesn't return. Someone may start looking."

Villa brought the cigar to his lips and breathed a cloud of smoke from his nose. And then he tapped the cigar ash onto his desk.

"Who," he said, "will look for an orphan?"

He waved his hand toward Dorotea.

"You make room for her in your tent. She cannot sleep with the soldiers."

He picked up his gun and walked back to the rat table. Our meeting seemed to have ended. One of the men lifted his big rifle and pointed it toward the tent flap.

"The *General* is now busy," he said.

◆

I felt a tug on my dress. Dorotea was standing very close to me.

"What is your name?" she asked, but my throat was too swelled up to let out a sound. "I had a nanny who taught me your speaking," she said. "You have spots on your face, and she had them too."

"Freckles," I said, the word sticking painfully.

Dorotea laughed. "That is a funny name," she said. "I like it."

I shook my head. "My name," I said slowly, "is Rose."

"Rrrosa," she said, tumbling the R. "There is a flower called *rosa*. It smells nice. You do not, but I'll put some of my perfume on your neck and you will. You will like that, Rosa, yes?"

She took my hand in hers.

"Come with me, okay?" she said, and then pointed from me to the tent opening, like I was simple. Her fingernails were sharp on my palm.

I turned for a last look at Al. "Well, girl," he said, "seems like you're fixing to have yourself a proper adventure."

Chapter 15.

Dorotea pulled me down a long row of dusty tents. We passed a flock of chickens and a big cannon on wheels, and a rough-coated dog followed us, sniffing. The last tent in the row had bright pink ribbons hanging from the front of it. She stopped there and pulled me through the flaps.

The inside of Dorotea's tent was a colorful place. Bright cloths draped a pair of wooden beds, and a red and green rug spread across the canvas floor. There was a brass-bound trunk between the beds, and it had a high stack of books piled on top of it. Beside it was a small oaken dresser, and propped against the dresser's mirror was a large painting of a blue-robed woman holding a baby. I thought this was an image of Dorotea and her mother, until I noticed the two were wearing yellow crowns. The picture's frame had a strange glitter, which was caused by a thick studding of metal charms.

In the corner of the tent sat a dark-tanned woman who was sewing in a circle of light offered by a small window in the canvas. There was a tiny brown dog at her feet. It looked up at us and growled.

The woman gestured to me and shook her head. She said something in Spanish and Dorotea said something back, then stamped her good foot and shook her head too. The woman said something else. Dorotea shuffled her bad foot and made a pouty face, like she was about to cry. The woman sighed and got up from the chair.

She held up her sewing. It was a red dress with frilly green trim running around the neckline and hem. Dorotea clapped her hands.

"It is so beautiful, Rosa, is it not? Now that you are my friend, Juanita will sew for you too!"

She spoke again in Spanish to Juanita. Juanita made a frowning face in reply.

"You sleep here right next to me," Dorotea said. "Juanita will go for a cot."

She sat down on the smaller wooden bed and started tugging at the straps that surrounded her leg. "No, no, no," Juanita said, but Dorotea ignored her. "It is good to talk English," she said. "We can stay up all night talking if we wish, and we can talk about Juanita! Did you bring a doll? I have an extra if you did not. She was my favorite until my other dog named Lilo ran off with her and ripped her face. I will look for her." She stopped fussing with the brace and limped over to the trunk, pushed the books to the floor, and began to pull things out of it.

Dorotea thought I was a little girl, like her. Stay up all night if we wish! But I did not wish. There was nothing at that moment that I wished for, other than to go back home. A feeling of sorrow settled on me like a smothering blanket. I surely had no interest in strangling my hair with ribbons or bloodying my fingers with a stitchery needle, but I'd never felt less like playing children's games in my entire life.

And suddenly I'd also never felt less able to stand. My legs had gone shaky as soup noodles. I tried to move them toward the bed.

"Dorotea," I said. But she didn't appear to hear me. She made a happy cry and pulled a dirty rag doll with jagged stitch marks on her cheek and tattered brown braids from the trunk. She tucked it under her arm and then turned to the dresser and took a beautiful china-headed doll from the top of it.

"Yours is Araminta. This one is Catalina. She is mine, yes?" Dorotea said. She stroked Catalina's dark, flossy hair. "I touch her and nobody else." When I nodded, my head felt like it was about to roll from my neck. And when I reached for Araminta, I became a rag doll myself and tumbled bonelessly to the ground.

◆

There was a feeling of cold on my head, then wet.

I heard a garble of words, rapid and angry.

Then someone's hands were turning my head from side to side. I struggled against them.

"Easy, now!" It was a man's voice, speaking English with an accent like mine. But the voice was not Abraham's.

A bottle was pressed to my lips. Water, water, cold and

quenching, spilled down my throat. I gulped it like a thirsty dog.

I felt the softness of a bed beneath me, and then I heard Dorotea's voice. I opened my eyes.

Her face looked frightened. "Rosa!" she said. "You fell on the ground!"

"She's come a long way in the heat, Dorotea," the man said. "She's going to need to rest a while."

"But we were playing," Dorotea said.

"Soon you will play more," the man said. "After supper. Now, she rests."

The man was tall, with light hair, and when he bent toward me I could see he had green eyes like my father's.

"Young girl, are you hungry?" He was holding out a paper roll of candies. Dorotea regarded it greedily.

It was Juanita's hand that was pressing the cloth to my face. She spoke to Dorotea, and took her hand and tugged.

"*Noooooo!*" Dorotea wailed. She pulled away from Juanita's grasp and pushed against my side.

"Rosa?" she said. "If you get up right now, I'll let you hold Catalina. You can't play with her but you can hold her, yes? Just get up."

"Now, Dorotea," the man said in a persuading tone. Juanita shrugged her shoulders.

A wooden cot had appeared from somewhere. The man lifted me up and laid me on it.

Dorotea dropped the china doll onto my chest.

"All right?" she said. "All right now, yes?"

Chapter 16

The man gave half the candy to me and the other half to Dorotea. Inside the wrapper were donut-shaped sweets that tasted of sharp mint. I ate one and then another, and another, and after a few minutes I could sit up against the pillow. But when I tried putting my feet to the floor, the room began to move again.

"Just rest," the man said, and when he leaned close to prop my pillow higher, he whispered, "Don't let her boss you" in my ear.

Over his shoulder, I saw the tent flap open and Less Ugly enter. "*General* wants you," he said, gesturing to the man, who patted my hand kindly and left.

As soon as they'd gone, Dorotea snatched up the rest of my candy. And then she replaced Catalina with raggedy Araminta, and we played dolls. Dorotea did most of the talking, for her doll and for mine. "*Yes, Catalina, you are so lovely,*" she made Araminta say. "*Yes, Catalina, you are so smart.*"

Araminta, she informed me, lived on a ranch and had a lot of sheep. But Catalina was from the town of El Paso, and lived in a grand tall house with a balcony and a room just for books. She had a carriage and a motorcar, a pet chicken, and three ponies with spots. Her dog was a white poodle and her father was a banker, and she was allowed to comb her mother's hair every night after she freed it from its knot.

Dorotea offered the last of the candies to her doll, and when Catalina declined, gobbled them herself. My stomach made a loud growl, and Juanita rose from her chair and wrapped a black shawl over her shoulders.

"We have to stop now, Rosa," Dorotea said. "It is time for eating."

She took hold of my hand again and pulled me to my feet. She kept my hand in her grip as we walked, but my legs were still unsteady, so I didn't mind as much as I might have. The rocks were casting long shadows as she led me toward a large open-sided tent next to a pit that held a smoldering fire and big chunks of meat roasting on sticks. The smell of it was delicious, and a crowd was gathered around, eating from wooden bowls. Al said he didn't know an Abraham Solomon in Pancho Villa's army. But there were many men there. How could he know the name of every single one? Maybe somewhere in this crowd was my brother.

A group of women were sitting on the red earth surrounding the pit, bent over little stone troughs full of mealy dough. They pinched the dough and slapped at it, turning it into thin cakes they were cooking on flat stones laid over coals. The men clustering near them were tall and short, old and young, some just boys that looked even younger than me. A couple of them had ragged bandages tied to an arm or leg, and most were as dirty as if they'd been rolling in the desert soil. A man wearing a head bandage marked with a wide red-brown stain had to move aside so Dorotea and I could walk past. He nodded at Dorotea, but gave me a look that seemed to say he'd just as soon stick his fork into me as into the piece of meat in his bowl.

"Pay no mind to the soldiers," Dorotea said.

This ragtag group was a far cry from the U.S. cavalry soldiers that came through El Paso. Those men had crisp uniforms and shiny boots, and I'd never seen one wearing bloodstained evidence of recent injury.

Dorotea sat down at a table set up inside the tent. I was surprised to see it had knives and forks set out on it, and even glazed dishes.

"It is big *fiesta* this night," Dorotea said, "in the honor of Señor Juan Reed, who is writing the newspaper stories that are making *Tío General* famous in America." She drew her head up high and pretended to twirl an elegant moustache.

"*Tío*," she said, "is already *importante*, but now he will be *muy, muy importante*."

Juanita fetched us food and poured glasses of milk from a white pitcher at the center of the table. I didn't take up my glass. I could not have milk if there was also meat. It was one of our Jewish laws of eating, and it held true all year round, not just on holy days.

"Thank you, no," I said, politely.

Abe would know how best to handle this kind of situation. But though I'd searched the crowd, I didn't see his face among the men near the fire. He was not in the smaller group dining at the table either.

"If Rosa does not drink milk," Dorotea said, "Dorotea does not drink milk."

I started to explain. "It's just that the meat…," I said. "I can't drink the milk because…," and then I realized the meat was an even bigger problem. It could have come from a cloven-hoofed creature, a goat or pig, and that was forbidden as well. I felt a sharp clutch of panic. *Say very little*, Al had warned. What was safe to tell Dorotea? What was not? Because there was no way to know this, I decided to solve the situation with a very tiny falsehood.

"Milk gives me the hives," I said, and pretended to scratch myself.

"It gets me hives too!" Dorotea said gleefully. She pulled at her sleeve, and showed me a red scratch on her elbow. "I have terrible itch, here!" And she pushed away her glass.

Juanita gave me the look thunderclouds make before the lightning drops.

"Dorotea," I said, "you must drink your milk, or I think Juanita will be angry."

"Juanita is always angry," Dorotea said. She stuck her tongue, pink and pointed, far out of her mouth and poured the glass of milk onto the dirt.

Juanita began to shout, and the two of them commenced a furious row. I didn't understand a word, but it sounded like fiery stuff.

One of the men standing around the fire came over to Dorotea. He wore a blanket and had dark hair, and so it surprised me when he didn't address her in Spanish.

"Little miss," he said, "are you putting burrs under Miss Juanita's saddle cloth again? The chief hears the two of you quarreling this way, he'll send her out to live with the coyotes."

Dorotea just scowled at him.

"Hey," he said, touching her chin. "Where is Dorotea's pretty smile?"

Dorotea tried to hang on to her frown, but as if she couldn't help it, her face lit anyway. "Señor Hicks," she said, "poor Adelita is lame, and she will limp when we ride. But if you let me ride your very smart horse, she will rest." She grew her smile even wider and added, "And for that, I promise I will also drink the milk."

"Young lady," he said, "you are forgetting what happened last time."

"It was something that will *not ever* happen again!" she said.

"You promise me?" the man said.

"I do," Dorotea replied, and she opened her eyes wide and blinked them hard.

The man didn't look convinced. "Let's review what you will not do next time," he said.

"I will not…shout at your horse," she said.

"What else?" said the man.

"I will not…hit him."

"And how won't you hit him?"

"With the bullwhip."

"Or the end of the reins...," he prompted.

"Yes," she replied with a dimpled smile.

"All right, then," the man said. "Tomorrow."

Dorotea beamed. "And my new friend Rosa, she will ride too!" she said. The man turned to regard me, and I had a sudden odd conviction his face was not entirely a strange one. He flashed a smile and extended his hand.

"Rosa, nice to meet you," he said. "I am Don. Do you like horse riding as much as Miss Dottie?"

"I've never ridden a horse," I replied, then remembered that yes, now I had. "Well, once. But I didn't much like it."

"We'll have to fix that!" Don said. I disagreed, but did not say so. These *bandido* folk seemed wild for horses. It would likely be best for me to pretend I was too.

"There will be horse riding tomorrow, *señoritas*," Don said, "but for now, I leave you to your meal."

Dorotea poured herself another glass of milk, and true to her word, drank it to the bottom. Juanita had filled our plates with rice, stringy bits of meat, and chunks of something orange—carrot, or yam. There were also some of the flat cooked cakes the women had been making.

Dorotea piled some of everything into one of the cakes, folded it, and bit into it eagerly.

My stomach seemed to think it all smelled delicious. "Dorotea," I said, "what kind of food is this?"

Dorotea shrugged. "It is meat and tortilla. You want *frijoles*? Some *jalapeño*?"

Unfortunately, my stomach seemed particularly fond

of the meat's savory scent. I poked it with my knife. "What kind of animal?" I said. Dorotea shrugged.

"*Jabalina*, I think. It is just meat," she said, and turned back to her plate.

My stomach made a sad groan. "Isn't that wild pig?" I said, and pushed away the plate.

Dorotea looked up again, smeary brown sauce on her chin. "The man called Samuel says yes it is. He does not like the taste of *jabalina*, but the men are trying always to make him eat it. That is why they tease him and call him Cerdo, 'pig.' It is a funny name. Should I call you Cerdo too?"

"Samuel?" I said, feeling my breath come quicker. That was Abe's middle name. "Can you point to him?"

Dorotea put down her fork and looked around the encampment. She even stood up to look a second time.

"No," she said. "Today Samuel is not here."

◆

It took a while for my breathing to slow. And when that finally happened, I still had to figure out how to get that meat off my plate. Finally I just knocked the plate onto the ground.

I made it look like an accident. "Whoops!" I said, and filled it again with just rice, tortilla, and vegetable. I found the tortilla chewy, with a taste of corn that was not unpleasant, and the seasoning of the rice was quite tasty.

Some men joined us at the table. Their clothes were not as dirty as the soldiers', and a couple of them spoke English in funny, foreign ways. The man who had given me the candy was among them. He placed a notebook and fountain pen beside a plate, then sat across from me and held out his hand to shake.

"I'm glad to see you're feeling better, Miss Rose. Allow me to introduce myself properly," he said. "My name is John Reed, and I'm a reporter for *Metropolitan Magazine* and the newspaper *The New York World*." I'd never before met a news reporter. His handshake was very firm, probably from so much time spent with his pen.

"People everywhere are hungry for news of this great revolution," he said, and his eyes bored most piercingly into mine. "Fighters have come from all over the globe to join with the Villistas, but there are not many young girls among them. Would you spare a few minutes to tell me your story?"

I looked away from the grip of his gaze. What was I to say? Al had thought it best to invent a fable about me for Pancho Villa. But I couldn't remember anything past the orphan part, to say nothing of the fact that speaking it would be repeating his lie. I shook my head. "I have no story," I replied.

John Reed laughed. "Modesty is not always a virtue, Miss Rose. Truly, it must have been a powerful urge for justice that led you from the comfort of your home to this harsh, desolate place where the only commonality among the disparate population is the desire for freedom and equality among all people."

He had a fine, curlicue way with words that made my own seem dull as bricks. I picked up a napkin and wiped my mouth with it, then took up my fork and put it back down.

"Perhaps, Miss Rose," he said, "it would be easier to

discuss your courage away from your friend." He stood up, held out his arm, and said to Dorotea, "With your permission?"

Dorotea smiled and turned to me. "You did not eat the meat," she said. "It is Pico's now, all right, Rosa?" She grabbed a strip of it from the serving plate and hung it over the little dog's head. He leaped to the tabletop, stood on his tiny hind toes, and snatched it from her fingers.

Chapter 17

I walked with John Reed away from the firelight, toward a cluster of big boulders the setting sun had turned glowing orange. This had surely been the longest day I'd ever lived, as well as the most distressing, and the only story my mind seemed able to conjure was the true one. John Reed motioned me to sit on a small boulder and took a seat on another. I hoped he didn't intend to offer me his stare again. Trying to keep my balance on the boulder was hard enough.

"Mr. Reed," I said, "I can tell you very little."

"My friends call me Jack, Miss Rose," he said in a quiet voice, "and I have a story for you about your brother." I had to stab my feet into the dirt to keep from pitching off the rock with surprise.

"I'm a journalist," he continued, "which means it's my business to learn all I can about everyone here in camp. Al told me you were looking for a brother named Abraham, which was a lucky thing because the man known here as Samuel happens to be a particular friend of mine. When I agreed to confidentiality, he confessed to me his full name."

My heart was thudding quite impressively. "He *is* here!" I said, nearly shouting it.

But Jack Reed shook his head. "Villa has sent him on an important mission to Juárez. I'd be pleased to serve as your guardian, however, until he returns tomorrow."

I felt a lift of relief so mighty, I wanted to jump off the boulder and dance. Everything would work out after all. I just had to get through one night, and then, together, Abe and I would go back home.

"Has my brother ever spoken of me?" I said.

"Of you, and of your family," he replied.

"Has he told you why he came here?" I said.

"I'm not at liberty to disclose that right now. But I do admit this is a question I've been wondering about you. What would compel a child your age to plunge headlong into the bosom of an armed encampment?" And he flicked his notebook to a clean page and leaned forward eagerly.

I had no interest in repeating the events of this long, awful day. "It was by way of an accident," I said.

He looked so disappointed I nearly wished I'd made something up. "I'm sure you're just being humble. Perhaps you'll tell me your story another time," he said.

"And perhaps," I replied, "you'll be so kind as to tell me some stories right now. Why does my brother disguise his name? And why did Al tell Pancho Villa something about me that is untrue? And why are you and all these people here, in the middle of the desert? What exactly is going on in this place?"

The sun had just dipped below the rocky horizon, and the sky above us was a smoky gray-blue. Back at the camp the fire in the pit was blazing brighter, and someone was strumming a guitar and singing. "Listen," Jack said. "Do you hear it?" I nodded.

"Do you understand Spanish?" he said. When I shook my head, he told me he would sing it for me in English. His voice was low and smooth.

Here is General Villa,
With his chiefs and his officers,
Who come to saddle the
shorthorns of the federal army.

Fly, fly away, little dove,
Fly all over the prairies,
And say that Villa has come to drive them all out
*   forever.*

The song did not impress me. It sounded like a powerful pile of hope was being heaped on a man with a sorry-looking army and a spoiled little girl who told him what to do.

"Who is to be driven out?" I said.

"It's much like the history of America," he said. "It is an uprising of the people against an oppressive, domineering government."

I knew just what he was talking of, though if Miss Polly

had been there she would have testified I'd slept through all of her long history lessons.

"Like that English king named George?" I said. "The spilled Boston tea in 1773?"

"That's it!" Jack replied. "Like the English. Though Mexico won its freedom from Spain many years ago, people from Spanish families are still controlling it. The Mexican campesinos, the farmers, work the land, but are not allowed to buy farms to call their own. So the campesinos live in squalor, work till they're ragged, all for the most meager compensation. Pancho Villa knows this firsthand. He was once a campesino."

"They're treated like slaves?" I said, and he nodded. Well, that was certainly something worth fighting to fix. Mr. Pickens had said such awful things about the Mexican people. I almost wished he was sitting on the boulder, right next to me, so he could hear their story the way Jack Reed was telling it. "And now," he continued, "the Mexican workers are staging a revolution, as great as our revolution. It's a mighty task. They were fighting General Huerta of the Mexican government. He had enormous armies, and of course the support of the landowners, but Villa beat him. And now they're fighting General Carranza, who started out as a revolutionary like Villa but turned corrupt. Carranza is a difficult adversary, but still, many think the people will win."

"My brother is not Mexican," I said. "This isn't his fight."

"A fight for justice is a call to every valiant soul," he replied.

I nearly laughed out loud. Abraham, valiant? Jack

should have seen him the time the Griffith boy called him a big-nosed Jew, told him to go back to his own country, and threw his schoolbooks over a fence. Abe didn't even try to fetch them back or defend himself—just took my hand and turned toward home.

"My brother knows nothing of fighting," I said.

"The Revolution has use for people of every kind," he said.

"What use does the Revolution have for Dorotea?" I said.

I heard a scuffling sound behind the boulders. A small animal with a long, hairy tail scampered out, snatched something from the dirt, and ran back to its hiding spot.

Jack gave a soft laugh. "She is as precious as a kitten, but clever as a desert rat."

"Dorotea is a spoiled-rotten girl," I said.

"She's a motherless child, very dear to Villa. Juanita is not always patient, and when it comes to Dorotea, *General* is not always wise."

"Is he her father?" I said.

The scuttling sound came again. I drew my legs far under my skirt to keep the creature from scampering across my shoes. It was louder this time, so loud Jack himself got up and walked over to the rock. But after standing there a minute, he returned.

"Come," he said, reaching for my hand. "We will go back."

And even though he still hadn't told why Abraham changed his name, I let him pull me to my feet.

◆

The sky had gone pure dark when we reached the eating tent. The roasting animals were gone, and the pit was filled with flaming twigs. Three men crouched next to it playing on guitars. They strummed a mournful-sounding song.

A group of women were dancing slowly to the music they made. They paced back and forth in front of the fire with slow and elegant strides, like they were off to a funeral and in no hurry to arrive. A man appeared among them. "*¡Animado!*" he said to the guitar men. "*¡Caliente!*" And just like that, their strumming turned fast and their voices shed the sadness. The women's steps became quick, excited. Their faces glowed in the firelight, and their skirts rippled and swung. The man took the arm of one woman and spun her around. He moved to the next and then the next. They danced faster and faster, like leaves blown by wind. When the dancing man laughed, he showed teeth the color of dusty shoes.

"*General* loves a *fiesta*," Jack said.

More men joined in the dancing. They paired with the women and moved through a series of steps so smoothly, it looked as easy as breathing.

"These people have suffered a long, long time," Jack said. "It isn't only a country that dreams of shedding a past and inventing a future, it is each and every one of its people, as well."

That Jack was certainly one endlessly high-minded fellow.

A volley of gunshots exploded behind us. Two men wearing fancy, huge-brimmed hats were shooting rifles into the sky. They laughed and shouted with happy voices, but it was still hard to convince my legs there was no need to run for my life.

One of the men called to Pancho Villa. Villa shook his head and held his hands up in front of him. "They're asking him for a speech," Jack said, "but he won't do it without preparing. He didn't have much formal education, so speech-writing is a job he usually leaves for your brother, who has a powerfully fine way with words."

A fine way with words! It was only because I was tired that I didn't tell Jack exactly what I thought of Abe's gift of false gab.

The men shot their guns again and hooted. I heard a bullet whiz by my left ear. I clutched at Jack's arm, and I confess I did so with a scream, but he just pulled me closer to the fire and kept talking like nothing had happened.

"Oh, Rose, the stories I could tell you of the people who come to join Villa's army. Some of what they say about their lives is very fantastic, but I think some of what they don't say may be even more so." He tucked his notebook under his arm and pointed across the fire pit. "Like the lady dancing with *El General*."

I looked closely at the woman by Villa's side. Her hair was pale brown where it wasn't silver, and she wore it in two long plaits, which, because of her age, would have shocked my mother. Her hat hung on her back and her dress was deep brown, not bright like the other women's dresses, and it had only a few dirty spots. Pancho Villa seemed to be teaching her the steps, and she laughed loudly when she stumbled.

"There are a quite a few women soldiers; the men call them *soldaderas*. But this one, she is different. She is American, and her first name is Audie," Jack said. "She will not give me her last. Audie says she's a widow lady, and had a chicken farm in California. But she has a way with a gun that you can't learn from shooting hawks and coyotes. She is the sister of Al, whom you've already encountered." Al was crouched by the fire, watching the dancers. He was without his hat, showing thick, short-cropped hair, and looked grumpy, like he'd prefer his sister was doing something other than dancing.

"Al knows guns too, and is even more reticent about the past than Audie," Jack said.

He gestured to a group of men in front of us. They were crowded close, drinking from long-necked bottles. I recognized some of them from the tent at dinner.

"Some Englishmen and more Americans," he said. "That one with the shiny boots is named Oscar Creighton. He says he used to rob bank vaults in San Francisco, but I suspect he's mostly bluster." Oscar had a large, bony brow, and dark eyes that shifted uneasily beneath it.

"The one in the black hat is Tex O'Reilly," Jack continued. "He told me he had a big ranch in San Antonio until a drought killed his sheep." Tex wore the longest moustache I'd ever seen. Underneath was a mouth that looked like the sun had baked the smile right out of it. "The rest of those men there," Jack said, "are barnstormers. You know—they fly aeroplanes."

"Truly?" I said, hardly believing him. I'd only seen the machines in newsreels. "Are their planes here too?"

"They say they'll bring them later," Jack said. "But Wild Bill Heath, the bearded one, declares he has hidden his flying machine nearby." Wild Bill was shaggy and rough, like the mountain men who came into El Paso to trade. He didn't resemble any of the handsome fliers in the newsreels I'd seen.

"The short round one's Mickey McQuire," Jack continued, "the one with the big pocket watch is Cyril Snyder, and that skinny fellow goes by the name of Farnum T. Fish." The men surely had the names of fliers, but only Cyril Snyder fit the looking part. He was taller than the rest, with pale yellow hair that sailed across his face in a crisp wave, and prominent eyebrows. The eyes beneath them were squinty and small, but Anna Rooney would have still thought him a fine-looking fellow. The sight of him would probably have made her weak and giggly.

"Are those their true names?" I said. "I can't imagine any mother wanting to kiss a baby she'd named Farnum Fish."

One of the men turned toward us to throw his bottle into the fire and called out, "Reed! Make me famous!"

"Free the Mexican nation, Mickey, and I'll be happy to!" Jack called back.

The men laughed. "You ready to take a ride with me?" the one with the wild beard said.

"Any time you say!" Jack replied. He said it in a shouting voice, like he was truly excited over the prospect of heading into a sky in a rickety motorcar with paper wings. Jack Reed was a strange fellow indeed. He had soft, smooth hands, and his shirts, though dusty, were far finer than I'd seen on anyone else at the camp. Jack was closer to a gentleman than a bandit or revolutionary. But here he was, in a bandit's den, and though he said it was for his employment, I suspected it was mainly because he really wanted to be. And in spite of all he'd told me about people's revolutions and freedom, I could not for the life of me understand why.

Chapter 18

Sitting near the fire made me feel warm enough to know I was very, very tired. But the night air in the desert blows as cold as its daytime sun beats hot, and the part of me that didn't face the flames was just about frozen.

It didn't seem like anyone else felt the chill. Especially not Pancho Villa. He was still whirling to the music when Juanita finally escorted Dorotea and me back to the tent for sleep. In spite of the late hour, the musicians continued their wild strumming, and sprays of happy gunshot were still splitting open the night. The gunfire caused Juanita to scowl and mutter. She seemed to be one of the few in the camp who hadn't traded common sense for revolutionary passion.

The noise was so loud, I didn't know how I would ever get a bit of rest. With the blanket and long nightdress Juanita gave me I was warm enough on my cot, but my eyes would not stay shut. I tried humming to help me sleep, but the only tunes that came were the ones from *The Mikado,* and they demanded singing. I thought I was singing them quietly enough, but when I stopped, I heard Dorotea's voice.

"Keep going, Rosa," she said. "Your voice is far more fine than Juanita's."

I sang her every song I remembered, and then some. I made up a song about the desert that included the phrase "the fact is, you practice avoiding a cactus," and the next thing I knew, the tent had filled with morning light. My back felt stiff and achy, and there was an odd feeling on my chest, a tremble. I rubbed my eyes to clear them and saw a pair of staring brown eyes. Below them were a wet black nose and bristling whiskers, and the rest of the face belonging to Pico the dog. He was wearing a tiny white satin suit and a matching hat, and shaking all over like he was freezing to death.

"Get off!" I said, and put my hands up to move him. He shrank his lips back from his fangs and made a big dog's growl. I heard a giggle next to my cot.

"I have come to wake you, Rosa!" said a high, squeaky voice. "You have slept far too long."

I tried again to push Pico off. He snapped his teeth at my hand.

"Dorotea," I said, "please help me!"

"Dorotea is not here," said the voice. "I, Pico, am now your master!"

When I pulled my pillow up and held it over Pico like I was readying to squash him, a small hand appeared and Pico flew sideways with a yelp.

"He will not really hurt you," Dorotea said, rising up from the floor. "He is just jealous that you will be now my best friend." She was wearing a bright green dress with ribbons on the front, and her plaits were hanging free like mine. She had Pico cradled in her arms, and as she stroked his little pink belly, his eyes squeezed with delight.

"Out of bed, Rosa," she said. "It is soon the time we ride the horse of Señor Hicks."

Juanita gave us some fruit and hard cheese to eat, and stood over us until it was all gone. The sun was well up in the sky by the time we set out to the horse enclosure. I had a feeling of nervousness when I thought of encountering all the soldiers again, but it seemed that Villa's camp was not a place of early rising. Many men were still sleeping by the burned-out pit that had held the fire. We passed two soldiers smoking in front of Pancho Villa's big tent, and a woman washing clothes in a little stream that came trickling down from the rocks. I saw Jack talking to a man on a donkey, and three of the barnstormers lying curled in blankets. I saw no sign of my brother.

It was a rough path we took, and Dorotea walked it slowly, but the place where the horses were kept was not far off.

The corral was formed by encircling walls of red cliffs, and there was just one entrance, closed off by rails of rough wood. Many horses were inside. They were as different-colored as birds, only not so bright and pretty. But there was one horse with a copper-brown coat so shiny it looked like a polished penny. It had white stockings on its hind feet and a long white stripe down its nose, which gave it a proud, dressed-up look, and it stood away from the other horses, its wavy mane fluffing a little in the breeze.

Dorotea saw me staring. "Is he not *magnífico*?" she said. "That is him! That is Tony!"

She leaned over the fence and held out the carrot she'd brought along. A scruffy horse mob came over and scuffled for it, but she wouldn't give it up. "Tony!" Dorotea kept calling. "Come here to Dorotea!" But he didn't. Tony looked too vain about his hide to chance letting the other horses put any gouges in it.

A loud whistle split the air, and Tony set his head even higher on his neck.

"Afternoon, girls," Don said, and then he swung over the top of the rails. He'd brought a saddle and some strappy leather horse gear with him. He also had a long rope in a coil, and he spun the rope out, snapping it, which caused the horses to scatter. He whistled again and held up his hand, and Tony nodded his head like he was greeting him, and then that horse raised right up on his hind legs. Don beckoned to him and Tony began to walk, one, two, one-two, all the way to the fence. Don dropped his hand and Tony put his front legs back on the ground, then stretched himself out in a long, dirt-eating bow. Dorotea was giggling wildly.

"Now you can give it to him," Don said.

Dorotea pushed the carrot between the rails next to Tony's mouth. "For you," she said. His eyes rolled to Don like he was looking for permission, and then he delicately took hold of the carrot with his lips.

"Up, now," Don said, and Tony rose from the dirt. *Crunch, crunch, crunch*, the carrot was gone.

He stood stone still while Don set the leather on his head and buckled the saddle on.

"Who goes first?" Don said, pretending there was any question. My short acquaintance with Dorotea had given me a pretty clear idea of what her views on taking turns would be.

She looked to me, her eyes bright as Tony's shine, and said, "You, Rosa. You."

The breath whooshed right out of my chest. My mouth went dry and my heart started pounding, but I wouldn't exactly call it a fearful kind of flutter.

The horse was a great tall creature, and I didn't see any ladder. But Don just pointed down to the ground again, and again Tony laid himself nearly flat. And then, as Don politely looked the other way, I bunched my skirt up to my knees and set one leg over him. Don handed me the leather strap that went to Tony's mouth. "Up," he said, and Tony rose.

It was nothing like sitting on Blanca. Her back sagged like the weightiness of life burdened it, but Tony's seemed to swell proudly beneath me. Don said the word "walk," and the horse moved out with a feeling of smooth muscle, like a giant cat.

Don told me what to do, but mostly he directed me about what not to. Keep my feet in the stirrups, don't let them bang at his sides. Don't lean too far forward, don't lean back. Pull those leather strips he called reins—but not *that* much!—to stop him, and chirrup to move him faster. But his steering ideas made no sense. Don told me to put the reins left to go right and right to go left, and though Tony responded willingly, I could not imagine why.

Don tied the rope to Tony's leather headdress, sent him out to the end of it, and said the word "trot," which made him perform the very gait Blanca had used to pummel me to bits. But Tony's version felt springy, like sitting in a wagon seat. Still, I thumped.

After a few circles of this, I was starting to feel like I'd been paddled. My legs ached from clamping Tony so tight, and then they started to go numb. When my hind end began sliding left, I couldn't make it stop.

"*Help!*" I shouted, and with a quick signal from Don, Tony came to a halt.

With another, he bowed down again and I heaved off. Dorotea climbed between the bars and limped to the horse, her arm punching excitedly with each step. Don lifted her into the saddle and made the stirrups go short for her little legs.

Tony raised up and took right off with the jiggling trot gait, and bad leg or no, that girl sat as tight up there as a tick on a dog. No thump, no bump, no jiggle. Then Tony switched to a faster gait, one that made him tilt up and down like a boat through heaving water. Up and down he went, up and down, and Dorotea rode the waves like a little sailor. Soon she was begging Don to turn loose the long rope.

"Sorry, sugar," Don said. "*General* needs Tony and me to do a little scouting now."

Dorotea pushed her lower lip out, but when Don made Tony stop, she didn't raise any fuss. Don got on, and I moved the bars down for him and Tony to pass.

As they left the corral, two riders were heading in. They turned out to be Al and his sister. Audie was wearing a skirt that appeared to have been sliced in two to allow for riding astride, and the horse she sat on was a muscled creature that looked like someone had ruined his nice brown suit with a half-bucket of white paint. Al was dressed as he was the day before, in blue canvas pants with the leather covers over them like cowboys wear. His hat brim shaded his face almost to darkness, and his white horse had a sprinkling of spots that looked like an affliction of black-tinted measles. Don pushed at his hat when they passed, and they nodded in return. I saw Al's hat dip for a second in my direction. "Girl," he called, "I'm sorry things didn't work out as you'd hoped with Villa. Anyway, looks like you're settling in right fine."

"*General* says Al is the best rider in his army," Dorotea whispered as they went past. "And the long-hair sister is the best shot."

And suddenly there he was again, red-faced Shmuley jumping up inside my head. He would probably split himself apart at the excitement of meeting a genuine gun-toting, horse-riding woman. Audie certainly had no resemblance to the cross-stitching, tea-drinking kind of a grown lady my mother thought I should be. She was free as a bird, that one, and she was doing what she wanted to do. The thought of such liberty made my feelings rise up like bubbles of soap, but another thought pushed them right back down. I'd vanished from Momma's life without a trace. She would be readying her black dress at this point, because she and Papa would be just about to give me up for dead.

Chapter 19

Dorotea was in high spirits as we picked our way over the trail that led back to the tents. "Was that not the finest horse anyone could ride?" she said over and over. "Was it not, Rosa, was it not?" Listening to her was getting tedious, and I knew she wouldn't stop asking until I agreed. But even when I did, she just kept on talking about that horse.

"Rosa," she said, "you do not know how fast he can go. Tony has so much speed, he eats the desert miles like they are carrots!"

Her words slowed my feet. A fast horse could make short work of the trip back to El Paso. A fast horse could get me home before I grew ill from sunburn and thirst. A fast horse could take me right through the desert before anyone at the bandit camp knew he or I was missing. Abe would surely know of another fast horse. When he returned, together, we would ride away from this place.

All I'd need to do was learn to stay on. Unfortunately, if

this day's lesson was any example, riding a horse at speed would not be something quickly mastered.

Dorotea eventually stopped talking about Tony in favor of her next most exciting subject, which was apparently sweets. She asked my favorite kind and I told her chocolates. And that made her talk on and on about how long it had been since she'd had any, and the store she'd once been to in El Paso which had the finest selection of penny candy she'd ever seen. On and on she chattered about their spicy peppermint sticks, miraculous toffee, heavenly chocolate buttercreams.

Her words lit my thoughts with a small flame of an idea.

"Dorotea," I said. "I love candy too. Surely Pancho Villa would see fit to let us visit this place. It would take just a few hours and it would make you so happy." I was disgusted with myself the second I said these words. Jack had said Abraham would return that day. How could I think of leaving without him?

But Dorotea clapped her hands together. "Yes, Rosa, yes!" she cried, and shuffled faster along the path.

Juanita was next to the stream washing clothes with two other women. Jack Reed was there too, notebook in hand. Juanita was talking to Jack, but went silent when we approached. Dorotea said something in an excited voice to Juanita. Juanita answered with a scowl, but that didn't dim Dorotea's smile.

She took my hand and pulled me toward Pancho Villa's tent, pushed aside the flap, and yanked me in after her. Pancho Villa was bending over a map laid out across his desk that had the word "Mexico" written on it in heavy ink. His eyes stayed serious when he saw Dorotea, but his mouth twitched a little smile.

"*General*," she said, "my best friend likes candy, and we have none."

Pancho Villa stopped smiling. "What of the candy Leon got last week?" he growled.

Dorotea shrugged. "That was hardly enough for one, and I had to share with Juanita, who loves sweets like a honeybee. There is none left, and we need more."

"Felipe will get some when he goes to El Paso for supplies," Pancho said.

"We cannot wait," Dorotea said. "But we can go ourselves, to the place in El Paso with the candy of all colors."

My heart, which had taken to lying low in my chest, made a jump.

Pancho Villa drew his eyebrows down near his eyes and pursed his lips. One hand pulled at his moustache. "It is a long journey," he said. "I cannot spare a man to accompany you."

"*Tío*," Dorotea replied, "we have been in this desert for weeks. It is the dullest place I have ever seen. You cannot expect me to be happy without any pleasures. I am only a child."

Pancho Villa bent over the map again in a way that seemed he was dismissing her, but I noted that the fingers of his right hand began to beat against his leg.

"We can go ourselves. We will take the buckboard," Dorotea said in a wheedling voice. "I think I remember the way."

Pancho Villa straightened up quickly. "You will NOT!" he said, his voice thundering. "Little girl, what are you thinking? I have no time for such foolishness!"

His reaction seemed to take Dorotea by surprise. Her eyes went big and her mouth sagged in a way that made her dimples vanish.

In the long silence that followed, I watched a dull green lizard enter the tent and trace a wiggly pattern in the dirt. A round, wet circle appeared next to its marks, and then another one and another. Silently, Dorotea was crying.

Pancho Villa looked at her with a face of stone.

"*Tío*," she said in a small, cracking voice, "please?"

Pancho Villa's face went fierce. "I have told you no!" he said. "No, no, NO!"

Dorotea gave a tiny sob, turned away from him, and started to limp toward the flap. Her leg seemed to be paining her terrifically—she could barely put her bad foot onto the ground. She was almost through the tent flap when Pancho Villa said her name. He covered his eyes with his hands and slowly shook his head.

"You will go in the buckboard. Agustino will drive. You will make the trip quickly. And you will go to the candy store and go *nowhere else!*" He turned back to his map.

Dorotea's face lifted into a smile. Without wiping the tears that still wet her cheeks, she took my hand again. I was grinning too, but not for the chocolate meltaways and peppermints. My freedom had just been arranged, and Dorotea had done it. It was a far easier escape than I'd dreamed it could be—my captor was escorting me home. And just like that, I was struck with a plan for Abraham. I would simply entrust Jack Reed with my letter on the way to meet the wagon. Abe would read it and soon follow me. Everything was going to work out just fine.

We were almost clear of the tent when Pancho Villa called, "Wait!"

Dorotea yanked my hand and we stopped. "That one's hair will be hidden," he said, pointing to me. "Agustino," he called, and a man stepped from the shadows. It was Less Ugly.

"Do not let her leave until she is fixed so that her own mother would not know her." When we left the tent this time, Less Ugly was at our heels like a dog.

◆

Dorotea decided to be disguised too, but as a boy, and so she made Juanita run all over camp to gather clothes for her costume. She pinned her plaits back up on her head and covered them with a slouchy hat. She took a pair of long, loose trousers and cut them short with Juanita's scissor. She finished off with a ragged red woolen serape, and then she laughed and laughed at her reflection in the mirror glass. Pico hid under her bed and whined.

Juanita made a long matted wig from part of a black horse's tail and pinned it tight to my head. It did not look much like real hair until Juanita draped a red and yellow shawl over it. And then she held up a bright blue dress with a sewed-on border of pretty flowers dancing around the hem. She said something to Dorotea, and gestured from me to the dress. "It was hers but now is for you," Dorotea said. "Because the dress you're wearing is so dull and awful." The size of the dress was close to perfect, and it fit snug to the waist instead of hanging loose, like my own dress had. In truth, the dress made me look quite grown-up. As I turned in front of the mirror glass on Dorotea's dresser, I barely recognized the girl I saw reflected. And when Juanita rubbed brown clay on my face to hide my freckles, the only thing left of the old Rose Solomon was green eyes.

Dorotea clapped her hands when she saw me. But then she frowned.

"You need one more thing!" she said. She turned to her trunk and pulled from it a black vest decorated with flowers embroidered in a wild, crawling pattern.

She held it up to me. "For you, Rosa, a special present," she said. I pulled it on over my dress.

"It was my mama's," she said. "I give it to you because we will be friends forever."

Her words gave me a pang of guilt. The last thing in the world I wanted was to know this girl forever, or be beholden to her for a gift so precious. But it was such a bright and pretty garment, that pang smoothed right down again.

But Dorotea was not finished. She said something in Spanish to Juanita, who went to the painting on the dresser's top and pulled off two of the metal charms from its frame. "For you," Dorotea said. "A gift from the great mother." The charms Juanita gave me were in the shape of tiny hands. "They are *milagros*," Dorotea said. "Miracles." And she directed Juanita to take the picture down so she could show me the frame's other charms. There were horses, dogs, a house, an automobile, some angels, birds, some lumps that could have been body organs, and a flaming heart with wings. She pointed to the charms I was holding. "You say a prayer, you see? And it will help your hands not be so shaky and cold." She pointed at a charm in the shape of a leg, touched it gently, and then Juanita put the painting back on the dresser.

When it was time to go, Juanita filled a waterskin and tied Pico with rope to a leg of Dorotea's bed. I felt in the right pocket of my dull old dress for the letter to give Jack Reed, and then in the left.

Nothing.

It wasn't there. I had somehow lost my letter and Miss Polly's, both.

"Rosa, come!" Dorotea said, and she tugged Juanita toward the horse corral. I had no choice but to follow.

◆

Juanita brought along a large parasol, which shaded us a little from the sun but not nearly enough.

The wig was even itchier than the blindfold had been. Now, as Dorotea's trusted companion, I was permitted to see the landscape I'd missed during my kidnapping. Unfortunately, it turned out to be little more than miles and miles of scrubby brush and cactus. But some of the cacti were holding flowers in their spiky, roundish paws—yellow ones mostly, and some in pink. I wished I could have shown them to Momma. She was always talking about how much she missed the beautiful flowers she grew in her garden in Russia. But I'd soon be telling her all about them.

The wagon seat was punishing to my rear parts after

the treatment they had taken from Tony. The brownish landscape seemed endless. As a black vulture climbed in the sky above us, Dorotea tapped Agustino on the shoulder and asked him something. In reply, he held up a finger and pointed to the land still in front of us. Dorotea sighed and pushed against the back of the seat. "We are only just half-way," she said, and took a long drink from the waterskin. Dorotea might fret about our progress, but it was clear to me that the dry brown line of mountains in front of us were the very same ridges that wound through El Paso like an animal's spine. With every hoofbeat they grew in size. It was hard not to smile.

Finally there was the sight of dust on the horizon, followed by some low, gray lumps which turned out to be buildings. And then there we were at last, at the edge of the town of El Paso. *El paso del río del norte*, the Mexican people called it—the crossing place of the river to the north. It was a town guarding a mountain range, a town full of all kinds of people living all kinds of lives. A town full of my parents' life, a town full of mine.

It was not the true home place of my family, but it was the only place I'd ever known as home. I got a hot flush of feeling when I thought how near I was to where Papa might right now be slicing meat, Miss Polly grading papers, and my mother preparing afternoon tea. But I was very careful. I didn't let one bit of this feeling show.

Dorotea said something else to Agustino, and he nodded and drove the buckboard straight into the center of town. The streets he chose were all wondrously familiar: Montana

Avenue, Pioneer Street, Mesa Street. We turned left and passed right in front of the Brunckhorst Hotel.

When Agustino made the horse stop, I felt like whooping. We'd landed directly at Pickens General Mercantile and Dry Goods.

Chapter 20

Ugly Agustino fussed with the horse while Juanita helped Dorotea and me down from the buckboard. I was so proud of how calm I was managing to act. But when Juanita gave us two shiny dimes each, my hands, oh, my hands. They started trembling so hard I nearly dropped both coins. Dorotea noticed. "Remember to pray to Mary," she said. "And your hands will be better, okay?"

I just smiled wide and started fast-talking in response. "I love chocolate creams. Do you think they have them? I'm just crazy for chocolate creams," I said, and I ran up the steps to the store. As I reached the door, Agustino called out to us, "That one doesn't talk." But I didn't mind not talking. I'd find another way to communicate with Mr. Pickens.

The first thing I saw when I pushed open the door was a woman standing in front of the shelves of canned goods. She had brown hair wrapped in a neat bun, and was wearing the style of dark skirt and woolen shawl my mother and the other newcomers favored. My heart started to pound like it would push out the cloth of my dress. I nearly cried out *Momma, it's me!* But when the woman turned, she showed a stranger's face.

Mr. Pickens wasn't behind the register, but his mother was, a stroke of luck so great I hadn't even dared to wish it. Old Mrs. Pickens was a more congenial shopkeeper than her son, always chatting with Momma about the weather and remarking on how I'd grown. My disguise might have been able to fool Mr. Pickens, but I knew she'd recognize me, even dark-haired and missing freckles.

We settled ourselves in front of the big glass counter stocked with penny sweets. I looked right into her eyes and smiled, and she smiled back, as I knew she would.

"How much for these?" Dorotea said, pointing her small finger at a jar of yellow suckers and grinning so charmingly I could have pushed our dimes into her dimples.

I saw Mrs. Pickens's gaze travel down to the brace that showed beneath Dorotea's trouser leg. "One cent for two, but sweet little boys may have one extra for free," Mrs. Pickens said. I expected Dorotea to blush or bow or stammer thanks, but she frowned instead.

"If the candy is free," she said, "I want...those!" She was pointing to a jar of red and green sourballs. Mrs. Pickens nodded, reached into the jar, and took three out.

"Three more of them!" Dorotea said.

Mrs. Pickens's smile fell a little. She set the sourballs on the counter and went back into the jar for more.

But then Dorotea did it again. "*No,*" she shouted. "*I*

changed my mind." She pointed to the row of all-day suckers lined up under the glass of the counter. Mrs. Pickens pulled her hand out of the sourball jar and her smile flattened into a frown.

"Five cents!" she said, and held out her hand. "Payable first!"

Dorotea's face puckered, and she looked again like a human child, not a demanding fiend. One dimple winked and then the other as she worked to recover her smile.

"B-b-but...a free candy...you s-saiiiiiid...," she sniffed, her lips quivering.

An actual tear bulged from the corner of one eye. I was impressed and horrified, all at once.

But Mrs. Pickens wasn't having any of it. "I said one free *penny* candy, but that offer was a gift for the cute little fellow who asked me—not the greedy boy standing here now, to whom I will now give nothing without money."

Dorotea's face showed plain astonishment.

"But no!" she said. "I am really a girl!" and she tugged off her hat.

Mrs. Pickens drew in her breath sharply when Dorotea's hat hit the floor.

"So now I get the candy, yes?" Dorotea said, pulling loose her braids.

But Mrs. Pickens just firmed her mouth and pushed the dime back to her. "Boy or girl," she said, "and crippled or sound, I don't want to see you again until your mother's taught you manners."

Dorotea's face flushed fiercely red.

"Here is my money," she said. "I will pay!" She plunked a dime on the counter.

Mrs. Pickens looked past her like she'd gone invisible, but her lips were pressed tight. She smoothed some undistinguishable flaw from her skirt and turned to me. "Your money first," she said, in a low, mean tone I'd never before heard from her. Things had taken a sudden bad turn. But I knew I could fix them.

I pointed to the horehound candy right in front of me, flashing a smile as bright as my coin. Mrs. Pickens nodded. I handed over the dime and gestured to the jar, and she lifted out two yellow sticks. Then I grabbed Dorotea's money and pointed to the sourballs and chocolate creams. Our dimes got us handfuls of each, but instead of smiling, Dorotea made a sort of growling noise. I hadn't yet seen her in a rage, but I imagined it would be more than grand enough to get us thrown out of the store before Mrs. Pickens had a chance to recognize me. My thoughts spun with desperation. I had to do something to calm her fast.

I got my chance when Mrs. Pickens turned to fetch a paper sack. I put my hand into the jar of horehound candy, pulled out one more stick, and slipped it to Dorotea with a wink. *It is not stealing*, I said to myself. *It is borrowing until I am free.*

And then I turned my gaze full on Mrs. Pickens, who held the sack of candy out for me. But I didn't take it—I just stood there, trying to make my eyes speak the words I couldn't say straight out loud. *You know me!* they said. *I'm Sol and Bess Solomon's Rose!*

She set the sack on the counter and turned around to fidget with a stack of matchboxes. She seemed completely deaf to the language of my eyes.

In desperation I pushed the shawl away from my forehead, leaned over the glass, and jiggled the peppermint jar so the rattle of the lid would make her turn around.

But when she did, there was on her face the kind of look a person gets when a wild animal has gotten into their house. Her hands clutched together and her eyes darted toward the back-room door, but I knew that when she was in the store, it generally meant Mr. Pickens wasn't.

"Now listen here," she said in a wobbly tone. "I want you dirty Mexicans to leave this store right now." And then she made a step toward the back room and added, her voice rising high, "Do I need to call in my son?"

Pinch, poke. Dorotea's fingernails felt like teeth on my palm. She turned to Mrs. Pickens.

"We go now," she said. "And we will never ever come back."

Juanita was waiting outside the door, and Dorotea said something that sent her darting back inside. Dorotea got into the buckboard. "Come," she said, and patted the seat, but wild horses couldn't have pulled me back into that wagon.

I turned and ran back up the steps. I hit smack against Juanita, who put her hands on my arms. That's when I went hysterical.

"*Help! Help! Help me!*" I screamed.

I heard Mrs. Pickens make some kind of yell in reply. And then there she was, standing in the doorway. She was hefting Mr. Pickens's shotgun, and she shuddered it to her shoulder and lifted up the long muzzle. Unfortunately, where she aimed it was right at my head.

"Don't think I have fear of using it!" she said in a voice that was trembling. Her arms were shaking so much she could not possibly have shot me down on purpose. Unfortunately, she was swinging the gun so wildly she stood a fair chance of hitting me by accident.

"*Perdón*," said someone behind us. Agustino bowed to Mrs. Pickens and then put a finger next to his head and twirled it.

"She is *muy loco* since the fever," he said, and he grabbed my arms.

Chapter 21

I screamed while Agustino wrestled me onto the wagon. I screamed as he hit the horse and made it gallop. I screamed as we raced down the street. The wagon wobbled on two wheels as we turned a corner, where a man and woman were crossing. I caught a glimpse of their terrified faces as they leaped to the safety of the boardwalk. The faces belonged to my parents. *"Help me, Papa!"* I screamed in Yiddish, as I tried to unpin the horsehair wig from my head. *"They're taking me away!"* They turned to stare as we thundered past them, but soon they were out of sight.

I kept on screaming as we reached the desert and left my parents and my home behind.

◆

Agustino directed bad-sounding language at me as he whipped at the horse. He finally fell to muttering after the town had passed from view.

I rocked the wagon with my sobbing. Dorotea put her arms around me. "It is all right, Rosa," she said. "It is all right. Stealing candy is a bad thing, almost as bad as lying. But do not worry—I sent Juanita to pay for it. I know you were just trying to help your dear best friend, and so of course I do forgive you."

She touched my back with fluttery little strokes, then took the paper sack from Juanita and fished out a sourball. She pushed it into my hand and went back into the bag and found herself two chocolate creams.

I felt a wetness on my face above the tears. The sky had changed since we'd left. Dark clouds covered up the sunshine, and a breeze had started to blow. A few fat raindrops fell on my dress, and then a few more. Juanita pulled out the parasol and tried to prop it over us all. She managed to cover me the least.

Thunder rumbled loud, and it was followed by another sound, a buzzing, angry roar. I looked up to the sky, and out from a cloud came an aeroplane. It was yellow, with the head of a roaring lion painted on its side and the words WILD BILL HEATH written in flaming red. Dorotea made a screech, grabbed the parasol from Juanita, and waved it up and down, which made the horse, already dancing in its harness, just about bolt. The aeroplane driver seemed to notice us. The machine dipped its wings right and left and then climbed up so high it was lost in the clouds. I'd given up on seeing it again when it came tearing downward so fast there seemed no way for it to stop before hitting hard dirt. I pressed my hands to my chest. Juanita made a crossing motion in the air, and Dorotea clapped her hands.

I closed my eyes, but they wouldn't stay shut. Just before

the plane's bright nose plunged into the desert, it some-how stopped its fall. It pulled up to level, and then higher. And then it soared straight, straight up like it was flying to heaven, and flipped topsy-turvy. It wasn't a mistake—the plane righted itself, and repeated the trick three more times.

I didn't draw a full breath until it righted and stayed that way. And then the aeroplane flew down toward us, skim-ming so low I could see the flowing beard of the pilot and the passenger's windblown grin.

"*Hellooo, Miss Rose!*" the passenger called out. It was Jack.

◆

In the tent, I threw my horsetail wig to the ground. I had gotten myself home, only to be kidnapped back to the Villa camp once more. I don't think I'd ever hosted a sadder, more desperate mood.

Pico shook the wig wildly, which made Dorotea laugh. Her face was sticky with candy, and she couldn't stop talking about the plane.

"Did you see, Rosa? Did you see, Juanita?" she kept say-ing. "It went round and round and round!"

Chapter 22

There was no white cloth and no china on our table this evening, only crude wooden boards and bowls. Though the platters were heaped with steaming piles of food, the trace of candy in my mouth made me feel sick, and I had no appetite for any of it.

It seemed that more men had arrived in camp while we were gone; there were scraggly soldiers everywhere in sight, eating the tortillas as quickly as the women could cook them. They didn't come into our tent, but they crowded distressingly all around it.

But Jack Reed had said my brother would return this day, so I made myself look up and note the soldiers one by one. I saw no sign of him.

Dorotea sat across from me, gobbling her rice and feeding Pico red beans. She looked up suddenly and made a bean-speckled smile at someone behind me at the moment I felt a touch on my shoulder. "Good evening to you, ladies," said a man's deep voice.

My heart is a ridiculous creature. It tried to convince my ears those words came from the mouth of my brother. But when I saw it was only Jack, who set a bowl of food on the table beside me, my heart made a most painful flop.

Dorotea started talking so quickly her words jammed all together. "The aeroplane! I saw you, Señor Juan! And you went high and higher and then you turned upside downside. But you did not fall! You did not fall!"

Jack waited until she stopped for a breath to ask about our trip to town.

Dorotea was still as agitated as a spring-wound clock. "We got candy!" she said, nearly shrieking, "and I was a boy, and Rosa! Rosa was dressed like Juanita. It was so funny! And we got *so* much candy and we would have got more, but for that cross old woman and her gun." Her lips pressed together and she frowned, remembering. "She told us to leave that store. She called us *dirty Mexicans*." Dorotea repeated Mrs. Pickens's ugly words with the same awful tone.

Jack frowned. "There are some who show unkindness to others simply because they are different from themselves," he said. "It is just difference they fear."

Dorotea shrugged and moved her plate in front of Pico, who lapped at the rice. "I wish to tell *General* of the plane. And then, Rosa, we will find Señor Hicks. He has promised to teach us to make a rope dance!" She picked up Pico and ran toward Pancho Villa's tent.

As I watched her go, my breath escaped in a whoosh. It

was the first time I'd been more than a leash's length from Dorotea all day.

I turned to Jack. "Has he arrived?" I asked, careful not to say my brother's name. He pushed his plate away and stood up. "Miss Rose," he said, "would you care to take a turn with me?"

He took my arm in a close, confident way that would have made Anna Rooney faint on the dirt, but didn't speak again until we were beyond anyone's hearing. "Your brother has been delayed," he said.

My heart already felt like a stone, but his words made it hang even lower. "But when will he come?" I said. I managed to say it with just a tiny quaver.

"Don't worry, Rose," Jack said. "Abe won't be gone much longer." He patted my hand soothingly. And then he stopped walking. "This is something I should perhaps not disclose, but Abraham is doing very important work in Juárez. He's engaged in a dialogue with Furness, the American consul, trying to keep the U.S. army from hunting down Villa and his troops."

Some of these men were thugs and kidnappers. Hunting down was the least of what they deserved, but I thought it best not to say these words to Jack. "Why couldn't someone else go?" I said. "Like Agustino?"

"Agustino is good with a gun, but not as accomplished with a diplomatic turn of phrase," he replied. A group of men and women passed close to us, the men pulling at their hats in greeting. Jack touched his in return and we began to walk again.

"Agustino is a devil," I whispered. Jack smiled, with what seemed like sympathy.

"He is Villa's most trusted officer. What Villa wants, Agustino delivers."

"And what Dorotea wants, Villa gives her, even if what she wants is people." I'm not ashamed to admit there was some whine in my voice as I said this, along with some tremble.

"If you want to get away from Dorotea," Jack said, "you do what her dog did, the one that ripped her doll."

"What was that?" I asked, looking up at him.

"You make her no longer want you," he replied.

◆

We came upon a group of men gathered around a clump of rough boulders. They were cleaning guns and playing cards, and smoking thick twists of tobacco. Some were clustered around a man playing a guitar. They were singing a song that sounded familiar, and then I knew it: it was that *cucaracha* song from the play yard at school.

It must have been a humorous tune. The men would sing some of it, then break into laughing, then sing some more.

They looked about as rough as any I'd seen at the camp so far, and when Jack stopped in front of them, I tugged at his arm to make him move along. But Jack ignored me.

"*¡Hola!*" he said, addressing the man with the guitar. "*¿Qué tal, Dionysio?*" The man smiled and said, "*Está bien, Juanito.*" And then he added, "*¿Macuche?*" and offered some kind of cigar.

Jack shook his head, pulled his little bound notebook

and a pen from his pocket, and said more words in Spanish. And then he turned to me and said, "I'm asking why they've joined the fight."

The man Dionysio grinned widely at the question. As he made a reply, he moved his hands like he was pulling something over his head.

"Robin Hood?" Jack said. Dionysio nodded and let loose a stream of fast words.

Jack translated for me as he scribbled them down. "He says, 'Viva Villa! Villa takes from the wealthy and gives to the poor.' Dionysio fights so he can get a new rifle, and a horse and saddle that once belonged to a rich man."

Jack turned to a grinning man in a yellow serape. He asked the same question, I think, and Yellow Serape's answer made the others laugh.

"He said, 'I fight so I do not have to work in the fields,'" Jack said, and the man folded his hands behind his head and lay back against a boulder. "He says fighting is so much easier."

The third man had gray in his beard, kind eyes, and deep creases lining his face. He smiled at Jack's question, and lifted the silver cross that hung around his neck and kissed it. "Viva Villa, viva liberty!" was his reply. And then he said, "My children are always hungry. Villa has made a proclamation that every farmer will have sixty acres of land. I fight not for me, but so my son's sons will have land of their own, and never feel an empty belly."

A moustachioed man sitting beside him was nodding. "My babies," he said, "my small babies, they starve! That

President Díaz wanted us to work and work in the fields, and give the landlord our crops for himself. With liberty we will feed our children, and they will eat all they want!"

I was struck with a sudden memory. In Russia, Abe had told me, there was a law that Jewish folks not could own land. And so our Papa had to feed his landlord first, and with what was left, feed us.

"*Libertad!*" the man with the guitar said. "*Libertad!*" the others repeated. "Viva Villa, friend of the poor!"

They started singing the *cucaracha* song again, and this time Pancho Villa's name was in it.

> *Una cosa me da risa—*
> *Pancho Villa sin camisa.*
> *Ya se van los Carranzistas*
> *Porque vienen los Villistas.*

"What does it mean?" I whispered to Jack.

"They boast that Pancho Villa can beat Carranza's army without his shirt on," he said, smiling.

The man with the guitar spoke again. Jack translated his words quickly.

"He will bring us to freedom! And then I will do what I want, when I want to do it!"

The older man nodded. "Villa says he will bring us freedom, and it will be so. He is a good man," he said. "And all who are wise know that those who stand under a good tree are sheltered by fine shade."

The man with the guitar stood up and struck a pose like a town-square statue.

"A good soup attracts many chairs," he declared.

And then the one in the yellow serape jumped to his feet and swept his hat from his head. "If your favorite dove breaks free but returns, it is truly yours," he said. "If it does not, close the coop, because it has been eaten by a hawk!" And that got them all to laughing so hard they didn't seem to take any notice when Jack and I left.

The wind picked up again as darkness moved in. Jack had to write up his story for the newspaper, and he left me alone by the fire. I mightily wished he hadn't. I didn't want to find Dorotea, and the dark route to our tent past the soldiers was a path that lacked appeal. I finally found myself a sitting spot behind a rock that was high enough to block the wind and low enough to let the fire's warmth come. I hoped it hid me from anyone's sight.

But I had a good view of the clearing. After a few minutes Dorotea appeared there, accompanied by Pancho Villa and Don Hicks. Don did indeed have a rope with him. He began to play with it, making it spin dizzy circles, one way and then the other, and turned them bigger and smaller with a flick of his hand. This Hicks fellow was near as good as cowboys in the moving pictures.

Dorotea seemed mesmerized as the rope spun up and down, up and down. Pancho Villa watched her, smiling at her pleasure. From this distance, it was suddenly clear to me that Dorotea's grin was Pancho Villa's grin, her eyes were his eyes. If she'd had a moustache and trousers, someone might have mistaken her for the hero of the Mexican Revolution. If he were shaven and wearing a frilly dress, someone might pinch his cheek and offer sweets.

She didn't call him Papa, but Villa was without the smallest doubt the father of Dorotea. Did she know this? Did Jack? And if he knew, why didn't he tell me when I straightout asked?

No wonder Abe liked this place so much. Everyone seemed to have as many secrets as he did. And as many lies.

Across the clearing, Don Hicks threw a rope circle around Dorotea and drew it tight. She laughed happily. "*My turn!*" she shouted, then pulled the rope off and swung the loop over her head.

"Dorotea," Pancho Villa said, laughing, "you cannot throw the rope like Señor Hicks."

"Yes, I can!" she said, and amazingly, she was right. When she let go of the loop, it sailed through the air and landed neatly over Pico's upright ears.

She was no liar, Dorotea, that was true. But she was as bossy as my mother, and like Momma, most of her truths were the kind that left you feeling like a stick had poked you someplace tender. Holding back some truths had to be kinder than jabbing them into folks. It was also a whole lot better than just plain lying. Or was it?

People like Miss Polly didn't lie or poke. Instead, they bolted the door of their mouths and let out neither truth nor lies. But somehow that didn't seem right either.

Miss Polly said too little, Dorotea said too much, and Abe lied like it was easy.

I didn't lie at all. But which one of us was crouching behind a boulder, a prisoner? I was where holding to honest had gotten me.

◆

Dorotea threw the rope around Pico three more times before she tired of it. "I want to show Rosa. Where is she?" she said, and I crawled even farther from the fire.

It was colder there. The moon was still low in the sky, and the only light came from the needly shine of the stars. Beyond the flickering flames, the desert was completely dark. If I moved a few more steps away, I would become invisible to the people by the fire. If I took more steps, I'd be beyond the field of boulders. With just a step, and then another, and another, my feet would carry me away from this place. But to where?

The Río Grande and Mexico were in one direction, and El Paso was in another. In any other direction there was just more desert, but if I headed the right way and walked till sunrise, I might be able to make it all the way home.

I moved a little farther away, and then a little farther, just to see what it felt like. The more distance I gained from the firelight, the more shapes I could see in the blackness beyond. The soft dirt hushed my steps. Nobody but Dorotea would care if I left, but even if they did, they wouldn't look for me until daylight.

But it might take daylight to be able to see the mountains that would lead me to El Paso. I tried not to think about what would happen if I got lost, but I had to curl my hands tight to stop their fearful quivering.

I passed a stand of cactus and an ankle-grabbing clump of bushes. As I reached a group of low boulders, I heard a high-pitched howl that fell into a long, trembling wail. It was the voice of a murdering owl, most likely, or a rock-canyon wildcat. They could kill you with one halfhearted smack of a paw, Anna had said, and then drag you home to feast their kittens. I heard the call answered from another direction, and this one sounded louder and even more desperate.

Death by bandits or wild animals? And Abraham. How could I get so close to saving him, and just walk away?

I couldn't make my feet take one more step.

The wind rubbed cold fingers on my neck as the howl rose again and again. *You're aloooone*, it seemed to say. *Alllll allloooooooooone.*

Chapter 24

A man's voice came toward me out of the darkness. "She-wolf," he said. "A huge one. And hungry." A match flared and, before it faded, showed hands cupped around a cigarette, and faces. I crouched down low.

A woman's voice answered him. "Nope," she said. "Just a coyote. Young male, most likely. Makes for good hunting."

I recognized her voice.

"Now, Audie," Al's voice said, "you leave that poor harmless creature be."

There was a long moment in which the only sound was the wild noise of that animal's cry. And then the first voice spoke again.

"Aren't you that sharp-shootin' gal?"

The animal's voice keened higher as Audie replied, "I might be."

"Cyril is my name," the man said. "You may have heard of me. I'm a quite accomplished flier." His tone was plainly a proud one.

Al made a sound like a horse blowing its nose clear of dust. "Well," he said. "Aren't you something. I suppose the sun raises up every morning just to hear you crow." And then he gave another disgusted snort. "Fly all you like. The only thing that matters here is, can you shoot?"

There followed a silence so profound, even the animal stilled its wailing.

"You'll see soon enough, won't you?" Cyril replied at last.

Audie's voice answered him. "We're heading off to fight any day now. That's what we heard."

Fighting? *It couldn't be!* But then I thought of all those new soldiers and Pancho Villa's frown as he traced a line on that big map. And I knew that yes, it could.

"We'll show that Carranza something, won't we?" Cyril said. "Villa's got a tremendous plan."

"You been in a battle?" Al said.

There was a noise of spitting, and then Cyril replied, "I have not yet had the pleasure, but some of those Mexican fellows say we're in for some terrific action."

There came another snort from Al. "We?" he said. "You'll be flying up above it all, slicker than Dick's hatband in your fancy machine. At any moment, you could just wing off for calm country." And then he added a few more insulting comments about fliers in general and Cyril in particular.

Cyril's reply came in a very spiky tone. "Mr. Pancho Villa himself has directly ordered us to scout ahead. But if we're needed, we'll land and do what any man...er, anybody would do. We'll fight for the Revolution."

"We'll be fighting against our own country," Audie said, "if Pershing finds us."

There was a long silence. "Yes," Cyril finally replied. "General Pershing. I hear he's really got it in for Villa."

More quiet followed, accompanied by the sound of some crickety bugs.

Cyril's voice came again. "Excuse me for asking so bold-like, but how did folk such as yourselves ever get into this game?"

"That's a long story." Al said.

"I've got time," Cyril said.

"You might say we had us a rough youth," said Al.

"Rough, eh? Ever shot a man?" I thought Cyril's question was sort of indelicate. Audie seemed to think so too.

"It's not a thing a lady speaks of," she replied.

Al's answer wasn't as dodgy. "You might say we're no strangers to the sight of blood," he said.

I suppose Cyril had some kind of answer for Al, but their talk was interrupted by the sound of pebbles on rock. And then a new voice spoke.

"Has anyone seen the girl named Rosa?" a man asked.

I was so surprised to hear my name, I stood up and tipped forward, right into the circle of faces. Pancho Villa's was now among them.

"Ah!" he said when he saw me, and he smiled and beckoned. I had no choice but to follow him back to the bonfire.

"Dorotea has been looking for you," he said.

I could not confess I already knew this, so I just nodded.

He stopped walking and turned to face me. "You are her

friend and you make her very happy, and that makes me happy as well." His eyes grew shiny. He blinked them hard. I offered him a small smile.

His smile back to me was broad. "Is she not wonderful?" he said. "This child, she is…water in my desert. She is the bright star in my sky. She is my sunrise." A tiny, shiny tear slid down his cheek, and he looked so sad, I couldn't help myself—I reached over and patted his arm for comfort.

"Of course she is," I said. "She's a lucky girl to have her papa love her so."

His eyes told me instantly I'd said something very, very wrong.

"She has no papa," he said, pushing my hand from his sleeve. "The life I live is no life for the father of such a child. If anything happens to me, she will only have lost her Uncle Pancho. She will always have Juanita, and she will always have friends, and she will always be cared for."

I nodded frantically and spilled out soothing words. "Of course she will. Of course she does." *Of course, of course, of course.*

But they did not calm him. "It was hard enough to lose a mother, do you understand?" he said, making his hand into a fist and shaking it near my face. "She will not feel such a pain again!"

He turned from me and slipped away into the darkness.

And then I felt a hand on my shoulder. It was Jack's. "Miss Rose, I have to tell you—" he started, but that's all I heard because something hard came singing down from the sky and landed on my head. It cinched tight right on top of my ears, but that didn't keep me from hearing the wild laughter that came next.

"I have been looking for you all over!" Dorotea said. Her voice was loud and excited. "I am going in the plane! *General* said so! You will look up, and see me. I will be flying!"

She pulled the rope from my head and ran off toward the fire.

Jack looked with sympathy as I smoothed my hair where the rope had tangled it. "I know what you want to say to me," I told him. "There's a battle coming. Villa will move his army to Mexico. So that means my brother will not fight that battle because he has to bring me home."

Jack tilted his face to the sky. "Rose," he said, but he seemed to be addressing the stars. "The truth of it is Dorotea's grown fond of you. And there is talk that Villa will bring you along."

I had to speak the words myself to help them make sense. "Bring me along…to a *battle*?" I said.

"Not near the fighting, of course," Jack said. "You and Dorotea will be driven in Villa's motorcar. You will travel apart from the troops and be kept safely away. The entire army is moving camp, and that of course includes Dorotea."

"Can't *you* bring me home?" I said. Though I'd bet my left boot that Abraham would likely see a battle as the greatest adventure possible, even my foolish brother would not wish me near such a thing.

Jack touched my shoulder with a heavy hand, and bent down a little so he could look straight into my eyes. In the firelight his eyes were very bright, and the sight of them gave me a strange, uncomfortable shiver.

"Rose," he said, "I must witness Villa's battle so I can inform the people of America of his people's great courage. You'll be in Mexico a week or two, maybe three. When things settle down, I promise Abe and I will find a way to transport you back to El Paso."

And that's when I realized why looking into his eyes had unsettled me so. It was not excitement I'd seen shining there, but pure madness.

"My dear girl," Jack said, giving my shoulder the kind of shake you use to wake someone, "you're watching history being written! Have you never wished for the freedom to see a wider world? For something bigger to happen to you and your life?"

The word "freedom" made my thoughts fly to that fine afternoon of singing the *Mikado* songs with Miss Polly. She had offered complimentary words about the way I'd sung a song about springtime flowers, and the happy glow I felt from them returned to my heart once again. *Oh Jack*, I said to only myself, *I have wished. I have, I have.*

Someone threw more branches onto the bonfire. I watched the flames shoot up into the sky for a while, and then turned back to him.

"Please tell me. What did they do to that dog Dorotea grew tired of?"

He squinted up toward the stars again before answering. "They drove it into the desert," he said at last.

"What do you think happened to it there?" I asked. He shrugged.

"It was mighty accustomed to being cared for," he said.

"So the dog's freedom was a worse fate than its slavery to Dorotea?" I said.

"I don't know, Rose," he replied, turning toward me once again. "You'd have to ask the dog."

I woke the next morning with a heavy stone of dread on my heart and a screechy, horrible noise in my head. It was coming from Dorotea.

"Please, please stop!" I begged, putting my hands on my ears. I looked at Juanita for help, but she was bent over some bright red cloth in the corner.

"I like singing too, Rosa, especially when I'm happy!" Dorotea said. She was sitting on her bed forcing Pico into a tiny pink dress. "I am so happy today. And I have not one, but four reasons why." She held up Pico's paw and pinched one of his toes like she was playing this-little-piggy. "First," she said, "because I am soon going flying up in the sky. Sorry, Rosa, that there is not room for you as well, but you can watch. Two"—she pinched his next toe—"because today we will ride Tony again. Three"—she pinched a third piggy—"because I am finally leaving this place of hiding and returning to my home of Mexico."

Pico's teeth were showing, and he seemed to be thinking

about settling them into Dorotea's arm. "Hold still!" she said. "I have not tied your hat!"

He lay back again. "And the fourth reason"—she held up his paw and waved it like a Fourth of July flag—"because *General* has promised my best friend Rosa will come too!"

The sun was already shining hard on the tent canvas. I felt a drop of sweat track down my back. "Dorotea," I said. "No."

"Don't worry, Rosa—Pico will not really bite me," she said. "He likes his hat once it is on."

I swung my legs to the floor. "About going with you," I said, trying to make my voice sound less cross than I was feeling. "Because I cannot."

Opposition had its usual effect on her. Her lower lip slid forward like a dresser drawer and hung, plump and shiny, in front of her face. She believed what worked so well on *General* would work on other folk as well. But I was not her father, nor her father's soldier or servant.

Nor her friend. A friend would not have to stop herself from wishing she could push Dorotea's lip back into her mouth and secure it there with the dog's bonnet ribbons.

"Why do you say this?" Dorotea said.

"Because I have a life in El Paso," I said. "And I want it back."

"But Rosa," she cried, "you have no mother and no father, no friends—not even a brother. Here you have me, and *General,* and anything you wish. Do you wish for more candy? We will get as much as we want. Do you wish for a horse to ride? There are many. I gave you a fine vest. Was

that nothing? If you wish for a nicer one, Juanita will sew it!"

Her mention of the word "brother" did not escape my notice.

"Dorotea," I said, "that is not my life. It is yours."

The lip came out even farther. "But I wish you to go with us. If you do not, I will be so very lonely. Like before." She pushed Pico off her lap and pulled Catalina from her pillow and cradled her. "I say to *General*, 'I am a child. I want children to play with.' And he says, 'Soon, Dorotea, soon.' He says when the war ends, I will live in a fine city like a proper lady, and I will even go to school! But he says it and says it and still we are always in the desert. We go to Tamaulipas, Tampico, Corrida…and it is always the same." She traced Catalina's fine features, then drew her fingers through her glossy hair. "I need my friend Rosa to play with. *General* understands this. Without her, I am alone again and very…very sad." The lip actually trembled now, and I saw a big gleaming tear slide out of one eye. If I hadn't seen her cry for Villa, it would have worked—I would have felt true pity for the girl. Instead, I felt an awful rage. I got up from the cot.

"Dorotea," I said, "how old are you?"

"I am *nueve años*, Rosa. Nine," she replied.

"And how old am I?"

"You are older than this, I know.…Eleven."

"Wrong!" I said, with such loudness I saw Juanita's needle pause in the air. "I am thirteen years!" I told Dorotea. "Do you hear me? *Thirteen!* When my mother was fifteen she

was married. I will be fifteen a year from next! I am weary of playing with dolls. I am weary of playing at playing! I am tired of this place, and most of all, I am tired of you!"

The words came spinning from my lips before I could stop them. They were a bit surprising to my ears, and I could imagine they surprised Dorotea as well. I thought they would surely send her right into a screaming fit. But she just sat calmly on her bed.

"Rosa," she said, "if you do not like your best friend anymore, why do you not just tell her? You do not have to make up such a lie."

She laid Catalina down and stood up. "Thirteen *años*—no. The thirteen-year-old girls who have speckles, they cover them." She pretended to powder her nose. "And also, they are..." She placed her hands in front of her chest like she was holding oranges, then jumped them down to her bottom and carved curved slices of air.

"I know you are not thirteen because I am nine and already I am bigger there," she said, and her smile was full of mockery.

I don't know exactly what happened then. One minute I was standing quietly, and the next I was flying toward Dorotea in a fury. It happened quicker than I could tell it, quicker than I could stop it.

But I never reached her. Something hit my leg and I felt a pain so searing it almost knocked me down.

Pink-dressed Pico had finally gotten to taste my flesh.

Chapter 26

My screams seemed to waken nearly every soul in the camp. They came running into the tent rubbing sleep from their eyes, because they thought it was Dorotea who had screamed.

By the time Villa arrived, Juanita was already cleaning my ankle with a wet cloth. I scanned the men crowding into the tent, but neither Jack nor my brother was among them.

Villa and Dorotea undertook a fiery discussion. They argued back and forth, forth and back. At one point Villa turned and waved his arms in a wide motion like he was tossing something, something he was glad to be rid of.

I knew exactly what it was.

Finally Villa turned to me and said in English, "Young girl, I have something to say to you."

Pancho Villa's eyes looked dark as the deep middle of a pond.

"Dorotea's dog has been bad before, but he has never done such a thing as this. I tell her I wish to get rid of the nasty thing before it hurt her as well, but this girl is of the tenderest heart and she say no, no, no." Dorotea looked up at him with eyes wide. Villa put his hands in the air, then brought them down. *I am helpless*, his hands said.

"And so this is the reason I agree to give one last chance. One!" he said, and shook a finger at Dorotea, which made her change her look to tearful. He turned back to me. "And to you I can only make an apology."

The men began drifting out of the tent. Juanita wrapped a cloth around my ankle and tied it in place. As she gave the bandage one last tug, she looked up at me. And then, though it was just the quickest of gestures, I swear she also winked.

Chapter 27

After Villa left, Dorotea acted as if we'd been innocently plaiting each other's hair when her dog had taken a notion to jump up and give me a chew. Through our breakfast, she showed me her pretty dimples and said best-of-friends things in her Catalina voice. *"Don't you love the soft bananas? Isn't the weather delightful today?"*

We walked together toward the horse corral, both of us at the same lagging pace. My ankle started to throb, and when I stumbled on a rock, she took hold of my hand and kept it, babbling on about nothing. But I did distinctly notice that her talking didn't include the word "Mexico."

Don Hicks was waiting for us. He'd already put a saddle on Tony, and his glossy hide had brush marks. The sunshine made Tony's coat take on a golden gleam, and the warm animal scent that rose from his body was somehow quite pleasing. As I stood next to him in the corral, he rubbed his head against my shoulder. He was such a large beast but seemed so gentle. I touched him and my hand slid down his hide like it was smooth marble. When he curved his head toward me and huffed a sage-scented breath, I put my arms around him. We stayed together like this, and for that long moment I could almost forget every unpleasant thing about the camp of Pancho Villa.

But when Dorotea insisted I ride first, they all came back to me. "Rosa, you must!" she said. "It will make me happy."

"No, Dorotea," I said. "I went first yesterday. It's now your turn." She tried all her tricks, pleading, dimpling, crying, but I would not give in. Finally her face went angry red, and she folded her arms across her chest. So I folded my arms across mine. She stamped her little shoe in the dirt. I stamped my boot. And that's when Don Hicks held up his hand. "Ladies!" he said. "We'll let Tony decide." And he led the horse right between us and said, "Okay, boy, which one?"

I'll swear to it, that horse actually tipped his head sideways like he was thinking. And then he reached his big soft nose toward me and, gentle as a feather, rubbed it on my arm.

Dorotea looked pleased. "This doesn't mean you won," I mumbled as Tony bowed down for me to mount him. Don started him off slow again, and told me to keep my legs just so, feet this way, arms relaxed instead of stiff. I managed it all fine, I thought, and Don was smiling like he thought so too.

And then he sent Tony out to the end of the long rope and urged him faster, and my legs crept up, my feet kicked out, and my arms started to flap like the wings of a crazy bird.

Thump, thump, thump. My bottom, which was still quite tender from my previous Tony ride and the trip in the wagon, felt sore right off. But what hurt more was the look on Dorotea's face. She was smiling, but it was a smile of joy in someone else's misery. She was hoping I would tumble— but I wasn't going to give her that satisfaction. I grabbed on harder with my legs, and when that just made me bounce worse, I took hold of the knob in the front of the saddle and clutched it tight. And that proved to be an amazing discovery. Holding it set me firmly onto the leather. Suddenly I was riding along like a queen. I circled around Don three whole times without a single bounce. And that's when I realized that this very saddle knob was going to be my salvation. It would allow me to stick to Tony as he ran, long enough to escape clear across the desert.

My thoughts started shuttling fast. I could get up very early and take him and we'd be halfway home before anyone missed us. Though that would, in a way, be stealing him, there were plenty other horses for Don Hicks to ride. And from what I'd seen in the livery, these *bandidos* seemed to live by a different set of right-or-wrong laws.

An angry voice came ringing across the corral, interrupting my thoughts.

"*Girl!*" it said, "*You get yer hands clear of that horn!*"

The bold, bossy voice of Al bounced off the canyon walls in a way that made it seem like two Als were scolding me instead of one.

He was leading that poxy white horse, and his sister was next to him with her own ruined-looking creature. Though the face Al showed me was very cross, I didn't care. If I did what she said, I would bounce right off that horse. Al yelled at me again, even louder than before. "YOU HEAR ME?" he shouted. "OR ARE YOU WAITING ON SOMEBODY TO PRY THOSE FINGERS LOOSE FOR YOU?"

"It's the only way, you know," Audie called. "The only way you'll really learn to ride."

"I'll fall if I let go-o-o-o!" I cried as Tony trotted faster. I had started huffing heavily with all the strain of gripping. Plus, the sun had risen to the midday point and its heat made everything harder.

"Girl," said Al, "if you have no interest in learning how to ride that horse properly, then on the ground is where you belong!"

"Now, Al," his sister chided. "That's kind of rough."

"Pardon me," Don interrupted, tipping his hat politely. "But this young bit ain't been much around horses."

"That's plain enough," Al replied. "But she's on one now, so she may as well learn to do it right." He tied his horse's reins to a post and marched over to Don.

"Stop him!" he commanded Don. Tony slowed, greatly relieving my rear parts, though the rest of me suspected things were about to get much worse.

"First off," Al said, stepping close to me, "the horn of the saddle is not there for you to hang on. It is for the use of holding the rope against the pull of a lassoed cow. See any cows around?" I shook my head obediently, but that didn't seem to calm him.

"Next—when you can't hold on with your hands, you will have to find another way to stay on the horse. Do you know what it will be?"

"You hold tight with your legs?" I offered. A good answer, I thought, but he just gave a horse-like cough of disgust.

"The way you stay on, little missy, is by staying *put!*" he said.

And then Audie joined in.

"Al, you're just confusing her. Listen to me, girl, because it's a kind of funny thing. To stay steady, you have to learn to let go."

The sun seemed to be shimmering even hotter. These two were talking like they had sunstroke, or the fever you get from drinking bad water.

"You do what?" I said, as polite a reply I could manage to such an addled comment. Don pushed his hat from one side of his head to the other like he was looking for the sense of it too.

"The tighter you hang on him, the more he's gonna work on jiggling you loose," Al said. "It's not Tony's fault, it's just a law of nature. Show her, Audie." And his sister mounted her horse and spurred it around the clearing, scattering horses as she went. "Do you see her hanging on anything?"

Al asked me. "Is she grabbing leather, strangling him with her legs, yanking his bridle?"

And I had to say that she wasn't. That Audie lady had some age on her, but she sat up there like peace itself. It was downright impressive, like Dorotea's riding, which was a thought that made me want to stop watching.

"*Pay attention!*" Al yelled. "Now, Audie, what is keeping you from cutting free of that horse?" Audie made another circuit before replying, "I have absolutely no idea."

Al looked to the sky like it might contain the one thing that could keep him from going right out of his mind. "Try harder," he said.

"All right," Audie replied after another circuit. "There's a feeling like a heavy stone that sits in the bottom of my belly."

"Now try grabbing on with your legs," Al said. "How does that feel?"

"Like that stone broke in two and went to my knees," she said. "And I feel like I'm gonna fall."

"The natural power of gravity," Al said, and gave a little grunt of triumph. "If you get to working with it, it glues you in. If you work agin' it, it rattles you like a pebble in a jar." He turned to me with his hands squared on his hips. "Listen up, Rose girl, because what we're talking about could someday be worth more to you than all the gold in your banker's vault. So what are you gonna do next time Tony starts to jog?"

He looked like he might hit me if I didn't answer right,

and so I thought as hard as I could. "I'm going to…let go?" I said at last.

Al looked as proud as Miss Polly when I'd memorized all forty-eight capitals of the U.S. states.

"You're gonna relax to stick tight," Al said.

"Let go to stay on," Audie said.

"Rein left to go right," I added.

"Yes, that too," said Al.

We stood looking at each other a minute, and then he slapped his hand on his dusty pants leg. "Well?" he said. "No time like the present."

Don switched the twig he was chewing to the other side of his mouth. And then he pushed his hat back into place and shook the line at Tony, who wheeled out on the circle and started up that trotting gait. My hands went to the horn like metal to a magnet, but one glance at Al's face made me let loose of it.

"Don't forget!" Al shouted.

The very instant I let go, my feet jarred free of the stirrups and my braids slapped my back. That horse was shaking me like a dog shakes a rat. I did one big bounce to the front of the saddle and then another to the rear. *This is it*, I thought, and I pictured myself as the lifeless rat after the dog finally drops it. My body started going soft. And one second later, a miracle happened: I quit being jiggling me and turned into a piece of Tony. We were floating, I swear and declare it—absolutely *floating* right over the solid earth. We were leaves, we were feathers, we were high white clouds in a clear blue sky.

It was the most incredible thing I have ever felt. I swiveled my head to see if Dorotea was taking note.

And that small motion was all it took to turn me back into a clinking, clattering jar of pebbles. Before Tony's hooves made three beats, I had rattled all the way to the ground.

Chapter 28

The first amazing thing about the fall was that it didn't kill me.

The second was that I didn't get even one bit hurt. My body parts, anyway, though my pretty new dress suffered a good rip right through the hem.

I pushed myself up out of the dirt to the sound of Dorotea's laughter.

"But you must get back on, Rosa!" she said. "Right, Señor Don?"

"Dorotea," he said, "I think Miss Rose might have had enough for today."

And then came the third wonder. I realized I really, really wanted to get back on the horse that had almost just killed me dead.

I watched with strange jealousy as Don got Tony bowed in the dirt again and Dorotea settled on his back. "No rope, okay?" she said, and Don nodded. The second he untied it she grinned wide, pulled her good leg forward, and banged it into Tony's side. They did one fast circuit of the corral, and when they drew near us again she shouted, "*Señor Don! I promised I would not hit your horse to make him go faster—but I am about to take that promise back!*" And then she took the reins in one hand and snapped them on Tony's neck. He gave a little jump, and she aimed him at the bar gate and snapped the reins again. Tony lifted himself up over the fence rails, and his feet raised a cloud of dust as they ran off.

"Durn it! Not again!" Don Hicks said. He flagged his hat at Audie and yelled, "*Can I borrow yours?*" He hopped onto her horse and sent it over the rails right after Dorotea.

"Young girl," Al said, taking my elbow, "you oughta be mighty proud, mighty proud."

"You did fine," Audie said. "Although we didn't strictly mean *that* much letting go."

"Pay her no mind," Al said. "Now, since you're going to be a horsewoman, it's time you learned about the gear as well." He tied his horse to the rail and began to lecture me on its trappings. He took off the headgear and named it a bridle, and made me put it off and on that horse three times. He did the same with the saddle, and then we scrubbed his beast with a bristle brush and some twisted-up hay, rubbing hard on all his wet spots. After that he took care of that saddle near as well as he'd done the horse. I paid close attention to all of it. When Tony and I escaped, I'd have to get him ready by myself.

Al was wiping the metal spots on the bridle when he turned to me suddenly. "You're altogether a hard-gripping sort of girl, aren't you?" he said. "You just plain like to hang on tight."

By this point I knew better than to disagree. "I guess," I said.

"Our aunt who raised us up was like that," Audie said.

Al nodded. "The kind of person you try to unloose," he said.

"Though it was about as easy as pulling a burdock out of a donkey's ear," Audie added.

I was taking offense at their words, but I willed my mouth to stay closed, and kept wiping at the saddle's silver bits.

"How did you come to be in the livery, girl?" Al said.

A sigh started in the soles of my feet and escaped through my mouth. It seemed like years since that terrible morning in El Paso, though it had really been just a few days. "I was there because of a falsehood," I said. It was quite an impressive declaration, I thought, especially considering the whoppers Al told about me to Pancho Villa. But Al didn't seem to find it so.

"Well, don't pick yourself to pieces about it," he said. "A lie isn't the most awful thing in the world."

"It's not the best, either," Audie replied, "but there's worse you can do."

They were getting it wrong. They thought I meant *my* lie. "It was my brother's," I said quickly. "I do not speak lies."

Audie looked at Al, and Al looked back at Audie.

"Never?" she said. "In your whole life? Are you certain?"

Al put down his rubbing cloth. "Have you ever said you'd

do something you didn't do? Ever said you wanted something you didn't want? Ever told anyone you'd be somewhere in a minute and turned that minute into thirty?" I started to shake my head, but then I remembered my last day in El Paso.

He peered at me, sharp-eyed as a bird. His words were confusing. "Well," I said, "of course I might have once..."

Al picked up the cloth again and leaned against one of the fence rails.

"Rose girl," he said, "everybody lies every day, in a million different ways. For example, there are the lies of not saying. Like the time Audie asked me if I thought her calico dress made her look younger." Audie looked frost at him, but Al ignored it.

"And then there are the lies of saying. Like last week when Audie asked if I thought her new straw hat was pretty, and I told her yes," he continued.

"It's a fine hat!" Audie said. "Of course you liked it!"

Al looked down at the dirt.

"Well, I guess I'll just throw it away now," Audie muttered.

Al sighed. "A lie isn't a rare thing," he said, "and it isn't hard to do. It's as simple as someone asking how-do-you-do on the street, and you answer fine, thank you, even though there's a blister on your toe, a ten-dollar bill fell out of the hole you didn't know you had in your pocket, and your handsome new horse can't gallop faster than your grandmother strolls. I do it every day. I lie when I'm asleep, I lie when I'm awake, and in between times too. I'd wager nearly every darn thing I say is a lie." He crinkled his eyes thoughtfully, like he was thinking over his words. "Except *that*," he added. "Well, and that."

"And that too," Audie chimed in, in a helpful voice.

In their strange, rough way, Al and Audie were trying to be kind to me, that was clear, but there was too much about my situation they just did not understand. It was time to sprinkle truth on this conversation. Well, at least a piece of it. I cleared my throat and turned to face them both. "Not only," I said, "am I here because of a lie, but as a result of it, I may never be allowed to see my home again."

It was a hard truth to admit. As much as I'd entertained myself with plans to escape with Tony, I knew full well I'd never have the gumption to try stealing that horse, let alone get away with it. I was headed with Dorotea to Mexico, and once she got me there, she wouldn't let me go. And the whole terrible situation was all the fault of Abe.

A high wave of sad feelings washed over me. My eyes started to dampen. I considered rubbing them with my sleeve, but it was dusted with dirt, so I used the back of my hand instead.

I felt a tug on my braid. "Young girl," Al said, "you're telling us you've been mistreated by others. Done wrong. Ill-used. And because of what happened in the livery, I'm sure you've signed me up as a villain as well." He looked over at Audie, who made a sad face. "Well, if you talk like that back where we come from, someone will be sure to say this: If you blame other folks for all your failures, you better give them all your medals too."

Audie was nodding.

"They also had another saying," Al continued. He winked at Audie, who said obediently, "You need a helping hand, there's a couple of them swinging on the ends of your arms."

They were talking like my kidnapping and imprisonment as Dorotea's pet was all my own fault, and all my own burden to fix. "I have tried!" I said. "And it's just no use!"

Al looked as sympathetic as a stone. "My sister and I have gone a lot of places and done a lot of things," he said. "And if there's one thing we can say we've learned, it's if you want something, the best person to fetch it for you is you."

Chapter 29

By the time we finally quit fussing with the horse gear, it was well past the noon hour. But Dorotea and Don Hicks still hadn't returned.

I had to walk back alone. I went slowly, sore and tender on my outsides from the dog bite and the horse riding, and aching all over my insides from Al and Audie's words. I crossed my fingers that I would meet none of the rough soldiers on the path. And I didn't, until I reached the camp.

I heard them first, voices shouting in Spanish and English, and the loud, high noise of excited horses. And then I saw them, a great surging crowd of soldiers gathered in front of Pancho Villa's tent. Two men came out of it, dragging another man between them. He was the flier Cyril, his fine yellow hair flopping right into his eyes.

As they carried him off, the crowd spoke with angry voices. Some men had guns and were waving them. One holding a long shotgun glared at me and said something to the man next to him, who glared as well. I ducked my head and moved away from them, off the hard-beaten path.

And then a man in a black cowboy hat and a fringed serape stepped right in front of me. "*Perdón*," I said, wishing suddenly I knew more Spanish. He didn't budge. The word had come out so tiny he might not have heard it, so I tried again, louder. "*Perdón?*" I said. Still nothing. When I tried edging past him, he exploded with words so forceful they turned him an angry red in the face. He shook a fist at me and took a threatening step forward, but the crowd had now circled me and I couldn't get away. Someone pulled at my arm. I yanked it loose, and then I saw a gap and pressed through it. And I was clear of the crowd, save one man walking in front of me, but I was going too fast and flew right into him. We fell together, tangled—he on his back and I pinned beneath him. I beat at him wildly so I could get free, and when that didn't work, I gave his hair the hardest of hard yanks.

The man let out a howl of pain. "DANG it!" he said. "That hurts like blazes!"

He twisted to look at me. And when he said my name in a voice of wonder, my heart burst into a thousand flaming pieces. Abraham's face was a muddle of shocked and happy. He jumped to his feet, grabbed me up in his arms, and swung me in a circle, which proved useful for clearing off more of the men.

But he set me down quickly, like he'd made a mistake. "Come," he said with an urgent tone, and he took me by the hand and pulled. He didn't stop until we'd reached the rocks where Jack and I had spoken the very first night.

"Rose," he said. "Never could I have ever imagined that I would I step off my horse in Pancho Villa's hideout and find my sister. How could you possibly come to be in this place?" I had so much to tell him the words jumbled together, and he told me to start again, and this time speak more slowly.

By the time I got to Pico's bite, Abe's mouth was pinched with worry.

"This is no child's game you've fallen into," he said when I'd finished. His eyes were very serious. "There's more at stake here than you can understand."

"Why couldn't you just tell us the truth?" I said. "Telling Momma and Papa you were going to Brooklyn. Did you not think they'd write Aunt Rachel and she'd write back to say you weren't there?" He didn't stop me, so I kept going. "And really, Abraham. That cowboy lie? It just made things worse!"

For a moment Abe looked satisfyingly ashamed. "When you found that letter I wrote for Eli, I had to tell you *something*," he said. And then he folded his arms. "But the letter was private, not intended for you. And you wouldn't have seen it if you weren't snooping in my coat pocket, a place you had no right to look."

He was right. I had been snooping. Abe had been acting secretive and peculiar, and I wanted to know why. "But it's a good thing I read it!" I said. "Even if you didn't trust me enough to tell me the real truth."

Abe sighed. "Someday, my dear Rose," he said, "you'll come to know that truth can be a light and lifting thing, but it can also be as heavy a burden as a stone."

The man across from me seemed to be a wiser, wearier version of my brother Abraham. I dearly missed the old one, the one that would have kept on scrapping with me.

"So now what am I to do with you?" he said. "You've arrived at a terrible time." He looked past me, toward the camp, and then turned to check behind himself as well. When he spoke again, his voice was very low.

"They are accusing that man they've just taken away of being a spy."

"Cyril?" I said. "Well, that's plain ridiculous. Al said that fellow's all hat and no cattle; about as full of wind as a corn-fed horse. To hear Cyril talk, he doesn't even know which end of a gun to shoot and which one to—"

Again Abe cut off my words. "Rose," he said, "they found a map in his tent marked with the army's movements and notes of Pancho's battle plan. There was also a letter addressed to the American army's General Pershing."

It was too incredible to believe.

"Well, why would he have that?" I asked.

"Why, indeed," Abe said. "And the answer is that the U.S. government will pay money to know where Pancho Villa goes and when. A great, great amount of it. Far more than you could ever imagine." He sat down on a rock and dropped his head into his hands.

He seemed exceedingly torn up about the whole thing. I gently touched his knee.

"Is Cyril your friend?" I asked in my most sympathetic tone.

"No," he said. "He's not." He got to his feet again.

"But today, I discovered," he said, and his voice was quite grave, "that there are not just one, but two spies in Pancho Villa's camp." He pulled off the big hat he was wearing. His hair was damp and flattened. "And this came as a great surprise," he said, "because I had believed I was the only one."

His words had a profound effect on my senses. I heard a hum in my ears and the sunlight turned watery, and I sat down, right on the desert floor. Unfortunately I landed on something with prickles, so I had to stand right up again.

"Rose," he said, "what I told you about answering an ad in the newspaper for cowboys was true. I received a letter back, directing me to a ranch outside El Paso. I was asked a hundred questions there. Are you brave? Are you honest? Are you willing to take risks? Then they asked one more question: Do you love the country of America? And when I said yes, that's when they told me it was not a man to move cattle they wanted, but a man to track a cockroach."

"Then you are not a Villista?" I said. "You don't believe in the Revolution, like Jack Reed?" The disappointment I felt at his words was almost as great a shock as the revelation itself. Jack's babbling had grown tiresome, but I suppose I'd begun to warm to the notion of a brother who helped struggling people. Hadn't Abe heard of the bullying landowners? The mistreated campesinos? Those hungry, hungry babies?

My brother broke a twig from a bush and fingered its hard, spiky leaves.

"I came here to help them capture Villa," Abe said. "But that's not why I stayed." He let the twig fall. "I've come to truly believe in what the Revolution is trying to do, and in the work of Pancho Villa. His methods can be harsh, but I think he means to do great good. I can't spy on Villa anymore, Rose, and when I saw the consul in Juárez, I told him that as well." Abe's jaw set tight as he said these words, and he pushed out his chin. "Furness didn't argue my decision, and now I know why—another spy had been planted. But now that Cyril's been found out, the Villistas are suspicious of everyone who is not Mexican. I'm afraid there is danger here now for me...and for you."

Abe didn't need to spell it out. He meant if Villa discovered he'd been a spy, and I was that spy's sister, I'd be in a world of trouble too. But was he also trying to say something else?

"We'll leave right now," I said, and grabbed his arm. "While they're distracted!"

He pulled my hand away, then latched onto my fingers, gripping them tight.

"You need to leave," he said. "As soon as possible. But Pancho Villa needs me. I won't stay to spy on him any longer, but I'll stay to help him fight for the freedom of his people."

I yanked my hand loose.

"What about Cyril?" I cried. "What will they do to him, and what if they find out about you, Abraham?"

He tugged at his rough beard, avoiding my eyes. "I'll talk to Villa about Cyril, but, Rose...Villa trusts me, and I aim to keep that trust. I'm far closer to him than Cyril is, and far more careful. I will make sure no one knows I was ever a spy."

I felt a push of frustration in my chest. My brother seemed unable to listen to common sense.

Abe got to his feet.

"Rose," he said, "there is a chance…just the smallest one…that something…could happen to me. And if it does, I want you to know that there will be some money due to our family from the government of America for the time I served them. And part of it…well…" He fitted his hat back on his head and arranged his face in stern lines. "I know Papa and Momma have wished me to marry a girl of our faith, but you must tell them I would like some to go to Polly."

He had dodged my question about what would happen to Cyril, and that bothered me something terrible. But it was quite clear to me that the words my brother had just offered were about the most heartfelt and honest I'd ever heard him speak.

I heard a rustle in the thin grasses behind the boulder, and pulled my skirts together in case another desert rat decided to take a run across my boots. Abe seemed to note the sound as well, and went behind the boulders and parted the long yellow grass. But there was nothing there. Nothing there at all.

Chapter 30

The crowd had cleared out by the time we walked back through the camp.

We'd missed supper time, but there were scrapings of rice and beans in the pots, and a couple of soldiers still eating. "Never taste the meat here," Abe whispered to me. "It is usually wild pig."

I could not help but roll my eyes. "Well, thank you, Abe," I whispered back. "But I have already figured that out."

We spoke very little as we ate. The soldiers looked so sullenly at us, it made me afraid. Abe noticed it too. "It's as I said, Rose," he said in his most quiet voice. "Just as some in El Paso think all Mexicans are bad people, some here now think all who aren't Mexican are spies."

"Yes," I replied, just as quietly. "And some *are*."

As he walked me back to the tent after supper, I looked up in the sky and saw a cluster of gray clouds headed into the sunset like a flock of scruffy sheep, a squeezed lemon moon riding between them. Suddenly the cloud bottoms lit with a fiery pink glow. It was a fantastic sight—sunset and moonrise joined up together, the clouds painted magnificently with those last bright rays. I glanced away for just one second, and when I looked back the pink was completely gone.

Abe turned to go. But then he paused and bent close to my ear, and in a voice so low I could barely hear it, he said, "Trust me, Rose—soon you will be home again." Without him, is what he meant. And though Abe surely intended his words as comfort, they made me feel just about as sad as sad could possibly be.

◆

In the tent, I found Juanita lying in bed and Dorotea standing over her. She put a finger to her lips. "She has taken ill with her troublesome liver again, and I am caring for her," she said, and put a cloth on Juanita's head.

As Dorotea and I got ready for sleep, she babbled on about Cyril the spy, and then switched to how fast she'd made Tony run and how hard it had been for Don Hicks to catch them. But my own worrying thoughts were too loud in my head to let in most of her words.

I got under the blanket, but my eyes wouldn't close. I heard a rustle of linens from Dorotea's bed. "Dorotea?" I said.

"Hmmm?" she replied sleepily.

"Why does the American army chase General Villa?" I asked.

Dorotea sighed, and I heard a thud and a growl. She must have pushed Pico to the floor.

"The Americans like *General* when they think he is winning, and when they think he is losing, then they do not," she replied. Pico whined softly, and the bedclothes rustled once more as he jumped back up. "Juan Reed says it is oil in the ground in Mexico they really want. It makes the motorcars and aeroplanes run, and he says America will like the Mexican boss who will give it to them. And to keep getting it, they will fight whoever fights him."

◆

My sleep, when it came, was full of worried dreams. Dawn was just starting to peek through the tent flaps when I got out of bed. I pulled my bonnet over my head against the chill, and set out to find my brother. I had woken with a resolve to inform him that when I went home he was going with me, whether he liked it or not.

He wasn't with the soldiers sleeping around the fire, or the *campesinos* huddled near the boulders. I didn't see Jack either, but I did see Pancho Villa, mounting a horse with heavily laden saddlebags. Two other men were getting on horses as well, and they rode off together.

An old woman had started making breakfast. I took three tortillas from a pile steaming by the fire and headed back to the tent.

Dorotea was sitting on my cot pulling shoes over her stockings. "Rosa," Dorotea said when she saw me, "Juanita is still sick." She hooked the loops over the last of her shoe buttons and reached for one of the warm tortillas in my hand. She chewed at it greedily, and when she finished she pointed at her bed, which was covered by a rumpled heap of linen. "My yellow dress needs wash. And my sheets," she said, and she held out her hand for my last tortilla. "Pico made them a mess."

I didn't give it to her.

"You take them to the stream," she said, slowly, like I was a little thick. "You put in the water. You...wash. Like this." She made her hands agitate the air.

"Oh no," I said, even though I'd been helping Momma with the washing since I was younger than she was. "I don't—"

She got to her feet. "Juanita washes, and she can't now. Farida and Conchetta wash, but they are busy, so there is no one else but you. Here." She laced the brace onto her leg, limped to her bed and heaved the sheets onto the floor, then went to Juanita's corner and pulled a block of dark brown soap from a wooden box.

"And then you put them hanging. Up? On a line. They will be dry when you put them back on my bed tonight."

So I was now to be her playmate *and* servant.

Pico was under Dorotea's bed. As if reading my thoughts, he gave a soft growl.

I took the soap from Dorotea's hand. I gathered up the sheets and clothing. And then I took them out into the stinging sun and headed toward the stream.

Washing linens in a stream was a ridiculously hard task. The wet sheets were heavy as lead, and when I tried to gather one end to wring out the water, the other fell in the dirt. By the time I finally finished, every bit of my dress was soaked through and my arms were throbbing. As I started back to the tent I heard a twig crack behind me. I felt a cramp of fear in my stomach, and took a faster pace. When I heard the sound of thudding feet, my stomach twisted tight. And then I felt the wet cloth tugged from my shoulders.

"Good morning, Rose!" Abraham said. He was smiling the smile of someone whose sleep had not been fouled by nightmares. "Do you know what day this is?"

When Abe saw the answer come to my face, he laughed out loud.

Passover. It was this night. I'd written that letter to save Abe from just this sort of God trouble, but the stupid piece of paper had just dragged me into trouble too.

He saw that on my face as well. "We won't miss the *seder*, Rose. Meet me at the stream right before sundown. And don't eat dinner tonight. Just wrap up some tortillas and rice and bring them with you."

Eat by the stream? He was either trying to make me feel better, or had entirely lost his wits.

"Abe?" I said. "This sounds crazy."

"Rose, just do it," he said in a grumpy brother voice. And he smiled again, this time even wider. "But hide the food well! Do you hear me? Dorotea can have no notion of our plan." And then, before I could say another word, he ran off down the path.

Chapter 31

Juanita didn't rise from bed the entire day, so Dorotea insisted we stay in the tent to tend her. Illness, it seemed, worked to sand down some of Juanita's sharp edges. *"Gracias,"* she mumbled as I held the cup to her lips or wiped a wet cloth over her hot face. Every once in a while Dorotea would lay her head against Juanita's chest and sing low, crooning songs. Her voice was rough, but it made Juanita close her eyes.

When she wasn't nursing Juanita we played dolls, we played cards, we drew pictures of dogs and horses in the soft dirt with sticks. And through it all, Dorotea chattered endlessly. *General* had gone somewhere overnight, she said, and she hoped he would return in time to watch her ride in the grand aeroplane. They would go fast! They would soar high! Wild Bill would do the loopedy-loop for her three times!

I had never lived a day when the sun took so long to drop from the sky. But at last it was nearly evening, and we left Juanita sleeping and went to the eating place. Taking the food was easy—I brought an earthen bowl and heaped it with rice and tortillas for Juanita's dinner. When Dorotea was busy torturing Pico with meat, I scooped some food from the bowl into a cloth, which I quickly stuffed in my pocket.

Juanita was awake when we returned, and her eyes seemed less hot and bright. She beckoned me to come to her, then took my hand in both her hands and said something in a low, raspy voice. She worked so hard for me to understand that I didn't want to disappoint her. And so like Al had done with Audie's ugly hat, I nodded my head, even though I had absolutely no idea what she was trying to say.

Dorotea positioned herself by Juanita's bedside and began to sing a tuneless song. After a few minutes I told her I had to look for a handkerchief I'd left at the dinner table. I'm sorry to admit that speaking this invention gave me only the smallest guilty twinge. It had become clear to me that in Villa's camp the safest path was the one paved with lies.

I found Abe in the place where the water rushed loudest through the stones. He'd spread a blanket on the ground, and I set my package on it. He had brought some things as well.

There was a big wooden platter that held two egg-shaped stones, bits of a branchy weed, and a wet leafy one as well. "Watercress," Abe told me. "It grows farther up the stream."

He drew a long, thin bone, mottled red with fresh blood, from the pocket of his coat, and placed it on the platter.

From another pocket he pulled a green bottle with a dark liquid inside.

"They call it *sangría*," he said. And then he shrugged. "Tonight it's Passover wine." He pulled off his hat and set it down. "And now we begin," he said.

He took some of my tortillas and wrapped them in a cloth. He poured the *sangría* into two tin cups, and lit a thick gray stub of a candle and put it on a flat stone. And then he began to sing the same song my father's rumbling voice had sung at every Passover *seder* of my life. I joined in.

"For lo, the winter is past, the rain is over and gone. The flowers appear on the earth; the time of singing is come."

"Rose," Abe said when we were done, "your voice makes the song even more beautiful." It was the nicest thing my brother had ever said to me.

I thought I heard a sound in the bushes then, and I think Abe did too, because he looked long and hard at the scrub by the stream. But then he raised his cup and signaled me to raise mine as well. "We bless this cup," he said, "and remember that on this night thousands of years ago, an enslaved nation set itself free."

The *sangría* was weak, watery, not sweet and strong like real Passover wine. We dipped the bitter watercress in the stream instead of in Momma's silver tumblers of salt water, and when we came to the point in the ceremony where the matzoh was broken, Abe ripped some of the tortillas down the middle. He insisted on making me cover my eyes so he could hide the wrapped tortillas for me to hunt later, in the way matzoh is hidden for children.

"Abe," I reminded him, "I'm not a child anymore." But he just picked up the tortillas and started to recite the matzoh blessing.

"This is matzoh, the bread of freedom. Let all who are hungry come and eat. Let all who are in want, share the hope of Passover. This year, we are enslaved. Next year, may we be free. This year, our world is in conflict. Next year, may there be peace!"

The words made my eyes fill with tears, and Abe's voice sounded awful sad as he said the final part. He was thinking of those enslaved Mexican people, no doubt. I was thinking of someone a little closer to him.

He was snuffling some too. I was preparing to offer him my hanky when I heard a sound of tumbling rocks and then a loud splash. It was followed by a scream.

We ran to the stream's edge. In the water lay a small yellow heap with wet black braids. Dorotea clung to Abe limply as he carried her to the bank.

The pretty dress I'd worked so hard to wash and dry hung in soggy folds, and she was crying. "Stupid Pico!" she said. "We were playing a hiding game, and I told him quiet, but he started his noise and he jumped out of my arms. I tried to catch him, and then..." She gazed sorrowfully at her soaked, mud-streaked dress. I could see Pico on the other side of the stream, shivering in the warm evening sun. He lay down and started licking his paws.

"You were hiding there?" Abe said, wiping her face with a corner of our blanket.

Dorotea grinned. "My walking is slow, but my crawling

is fast, and I am such a good hider. You do not see me, but I see you." She giggled and tossed her braids in a wet, splashy arc. "And I hear you. Last night, by the boulders. And Samuel, Rosa is your *sister* and she called you a name of Abraham. You have another name *and* a sister, and did not tell *Tío Pancho* any of these things." A sudden cold gale blew right through my insides. She had heard what Abe and I had talked of by the boulders. But had she heard it all?

But Abe just kept calmly patting at her dress with the blanket. "So you discovered this about Rose and me," he said. "What else did you hear?"

Dorotea beamed at him, happy as a crow who'd stolen a shiny ring, and then gave me a sidelong look. "I hear I am clever as a desert rat. But I do not mind. I like the rat. He also crawls into secret places. He knows secret things."

Her face grew sly. "I know something *Tío Pancho* would not like me to know. But I know this thing a long time already. And I know other things too."

I made a quick, desperate glance at Abe. *What now?* my eyes asked him.

Abe still looked cool. "Dorotea," he said, "so you know my sister Rose and I are Jewish people, and that in our family I am called Abraham." Dorotea cocked her head and fixed him with her bright stare.

"There was a Jewish here before," she said. "He shot *Tío Pancho*'s big gun. He also did not like the meat, *cerdo*."

Abe laughed. "Yes," he said. "And what we are doing now is Jewish…a ceremony. Actually, I'm glad you've come, Dorotea. We need your help."

Dorotea leaned forward eagerly. So did I. Abe would have to puff some pretty fancy smoke rings to get us out of this fix.

He drew close to her, like he was about to tell a secret. "We need you to speak important words in our ceremony, and after, to find a hidden treasure."

"Treasure?" Dorotea said, her eyes glittering.

"Yes indeed," Abe said, moving so near to her I thought they'd bump heads. "It is a task that can go only to a child. And my sister, as you can see, has passed that mark."

Dorotea looked at me quickly, then turned back to Abe's intense blue gaze. She nodded.

"But there is one thing," Abe said, and pulled away from her. "In order to hunt for the treasure, you must first be blessed."

"Yes? Yes?" Dorotea said, leaning in.

"This blessing will make you an honorary member of the Jewish people. And when that happens, you will be bound by a vow of fealty. That is a pledge of allegiance from one person to another, and it means you must not tell anyone— *anyone* at all—what Rose and I were doing here, and what you have heard us say. Today and yesterday both. Do you understand?"

She nodded eagerly. And then, slowly, her bottom lip started sliding forward.

"But...but...," she said. "I don't know."

"What is it?" I said, in a tone more snappish than I'd intended. Her lips drew down and trembled. "I like meeeeat," she said, extending the word with a whine. "I don't want to give it up to be a Jewish person."

Abe laughed again, a quick bark of relief. "Of course not," he said. "You may eat whatever you like."

Dorotea smiled. "So I can find the treasure?" she said.

"First things first," Abe said.

He picked up the candle and held it high over Dorotea's head. He waved it in a slow circle and he said, "*Baruch hata adonai, elohanu melech ha'olum, boray poree hagofen.*" He lifted his cup of *sangría* and drank of it deeply, then intoned, "Amen."

He'd just recited the wine-blessing prayers over Dorotea. She was now fit to be sipped at a Passover table.

Chapter 32

Pico helped Dorotea find the treasure. Actually, he found it all by himself, and when Dorotea found *him*, he was licking the cloth that covered it.

She looked very disappointed when she unwrapped it and found only a soggy tortilla. But then Abe reached into his jacket and drew out a package wrapped in shiny yellow paper. Inside was a necklace with a fine-linked chain and a beautiful pendant made of a carved green shell. Dorotea and I both let out a gasp. As he placed the jewelry on Dorotea's neck, I realized it must have been a present for Miss Polly.

"And now," he said, "you must do the other job of the youngest child at the *seder*. You must ask four important questions." He sent me a glance and I gave him back a small nod.

I whispered the words in her ear so she could say them out loud. "Why on this night do we recline when we eat? Why do we eat only the bitter herbs? Why do we eat unleavened bread? Why do we dip our herbs twice?" She giggled as she repeated them.

And then we feasted on tortillas and rice and some tinned beets and boiled carrots Abe had gotten who knows how. He'd also managed to find some apples and a tiny pot of honey, and he cut the apples into slices and we dipped them to sweeten them even more. I slipped a whole one into my pocket. Tony would like that apple. He'd like it very much.

Dorotea ate our food and asked for seconds. She kept touching her new necklace and saying, "*Gracias*, Samuel, *gracias*." She was a child who had anything she wished for, but she thanked him for the necklace with such true happiness that pretty soon I no longer minded so much that it was not Miss Polly's.

It was one of the strangest meals I'd ever eaten, and the strangest part was that it was also one of the most delicious. It was the oddest *seder* I'd ever attended, and it was somehow also the most wonderful.

When the sun was nearly gone, we packed up and started back to the camp. We didn't encounter a soul as we walked the path, and I took my brother's hand and held it, then reached for Dorotea's. Abe didn't shake me free until we came upon a cactus growing right in the middle of the trail. When he went to the right of it and I went to the left, I called out, "Bread and butter!"

"Not for eight more days," Abe replied.

"It's what Anna Rooney told me must be said when you go one way and a friend goes another," I said to him. "It keeps friends from being parted."

"Really, Rose," he said, mockingly serious. "Now that you're not a child anymore, you'll need to quit those childish superstitions. Next thing you know, you'll be telling me your nose itches and that means you're about to have company." He strode a bit ahead and began to whistle.

And this next part sounds quite odd, but I swear it's true. As soon as Abe passed me, I was taken with a most terrible itch. I dropped Dorotea's hand and scratched my nose like crazy.

◆

The camp was quiet, but Abe walked us right to our tent anyway. "Remember," he warned Dorotea once more, "you have been blessed." It was too dark to see her eyes, but the moon gave her face a silvery glow. "I promise," she said in a serious voice, and she waved her hand over her head in a circle, just as Abe had done.

Abe gave a slow, solemn nod. "And now, Dorotea," he said, "I will give you one last thing." Dorotea looked expectant, like she was ready for more pretty trinkets.

But no. "There is a very important word known only to the Jewish people," he said. And then he raised both arms over his head and gazed up at the moonlit clouds. "It is," he said grandly, "the word *shalom*!" He made the word ring so loud it echoed among the rocks. *Shalom!* they called. *Shalom, shalom, shalom.*

Dorotea repeated it carefully. "What is this word?"

"It carries three meanings," said Abe. "One is 'hello,' one is 'good-bye.' The third is 'peace.'"

He smiled and gave a little bow, and started back down the path. And then he turned around and gave a half wave. "*Shalom!*" he called, but softly this time.

Dorotea nudged me. "*Shalom!*" she and I called back together.

◆

Juanita was sleeping quietly when we entered the tent, so we changed into nightclothes without disturbing her and got into our beds. But Dorotea was restless. I sang to her for a while, and when that didn't settle her, I told her the whole of the Passover story, including the enslaving pharaoh, the land of Egypt, baby Moses set floating down the river in the basket of reeds, and how the pharaoh's daughter found him and raised him as her own. I told her about the locusts and the other plagues, the Jewish people's flight into the desert, and finding freedom in the Promised Land after forty long years of wandering. "They doubted, but they never gave up hope," I told her sleepily. "They never ever did." It was fun to lie there talking in the dark, and the joyful feeling I'd had at our streamside *seder* filled me again. Making Dorotea happy was somehow making me happy too. Was it like this to have a sister? If things had been different, could she and I have been real friends?

"Rosa," Dorotea said after a long pause in our talking. "Is there anything you fear?"

I thought awhile before I made an answer. "Why do you ask me this?" I finally said.

"Because late at night I think only of things that make me scared," she replied.

I wouldn't have believed she was afraid of anything on earth. "Like what?" I said.

She sighed. "Coyotes. I have fear of them, for once I saw one kill a kitten. And lightning. It can strike you dead with just one pretty flash. I fear the bee, because once a bee stung me, and fish, because they are so smelly."

She fell silent. When finally she spoke again, her voice held tears. "But more than any of this, Rosa, I have fear of one thing." And she stopped talking.

I lay quietly, wondering if I should prod her or just let her fall asleep. And then I heard a muffled sound of crying.

"Dorotea?" I said.

Her reply was so choked I could barely make it out. "I am afraid," she sobbed, "of being in the world all alone. Rosa, I am so afraid of this."

I got out of bed and took her hand. It was shaking.

I squeezed it, pulled my breath in deeply, and said, "I am afraid too."

"Of what?" she said. Her voice was very small.

"I'm afraid of dogs and afraid of horses. I'm afraid of wild animals. I'm afraid of displeasing people and afraid of pleasing them, of being with them and being without them."

I knew I should stop, but the words just kept tumbling. "I'm afraid of being free, and afraid of being trapped. I'm afraid of the soldiers that surround us here. I'm afraid of being killed and I fear the same for my brother. And though I know there's no use of this, I am really, really afraid of being grown-up."

I felt a soft touch on the back of my hand. Dorotea had

given it a kiss. Her breath became slower, and deeper, and after a minute I slipped my hand away and climbed back onto my cot. Just when I thought she'd drifted off, she spoke.

"So that Moses man you spoke of was a spy in the house of the pharaoh?"

"You might say," I replied. She was silent for so long I thought for sure she'd fallen asleep at last. And then her voice came again.

"Like the flier?"

"Yes," I told her quietly. There was another long pause and then she said, "Are you a spy, Rosa? Is your brother?"

I had to make a couple of tries before I was able to push the correct answer back down my throat, but finally I managed it. "No, Dorotea," I said, with a firm tone Abe himself would have been proud of. "We are not." Strictly speaking, Abe had stopped spying, but my words felt like swallowed truth anyway. But then I remembered again Audie's hat. A lie to save pride—or a life—seemed far from a terrible, unforgivable thing. In fact, it seemed a fair bit...honorable.

I broke the long silence that followed with the question I'd been trying not to think of all day.

"Do you know what will happen to Cyril, Dorotea?"

She gave a sleepy yawn.

"If the man is lucky, they will kill him fast," Dorotea replied. "If he is not..." And her voice trailed off.

Chapter **33**

The first thing I saw when I opened my eyes the next morning was Juanita laying a blue dress and a pair of pretty white shoes at the foot of Dorotea's bed. She was moving slowly, and had one hand pressed to her waist.

Dorotea hopped from her bed and threw her arms around Juanita, and Juanita hugged her back. It was a happy, cheerful start that by contrast would make the rest of the day's unfoldings feel even worse.

I was anxious to tell Abe what Dorotea had said about Cyril, but he didn't appear by the fire that morning. When I tasted my tea it was too hot, and it scalded half my tongue. I tore the sleeve of the nice dress Juanita had given me on a cactus on the way to the outhouse, and then I stepped in a clump of some donkey's foulness on the way back.

By midday the sun burned down hot as coal in a stove, and the tent's walls did little to stop it. Crowds of tiny flies appeared from somewhere to buzz around my face, thirsty for the water in my eyes. I shooed them again and again, but they flew right back.

Heat, cactus thorns, flies, my brother. Everything was vexing. By early afternoon I had a headache too. I told Dorotea I needed to sit quietly, and picked up one of her books, but she was as persistent as the flies, and soon she was back in front of me, plunking Araminta on my lap. "Playing dolls will not hurt your head," she said with her finest dimpled smile.

She decided Catalina would be queen of the fairies this day, and Araminta her child, the fairy changeling. Because I was to be the mother of the queen, I had to put on my new embroidered vest, which caused me to feel even more sweaty. And then Catalina made me and the fairy changeling do every unpleasant task in the fairy camp.

Juanita's attempts to pile dirty clothes into a basket finally distracted Dorotea from our game. Bending over seemed to pain Juanita. She limped toward the flap of the tent, but nearly collapsed in the dirt when she stepped into the sun.

Dorotea went to her and took the basket, and led Juanita back to her cot. And then she dropped the basket at my feet and gestured at it. She didn't need to say one thing about what she wanted me to do with those filthy clothes.

I tried to recall the feelings of the night before, the way we'd talked, the secrets we'd shared. More than anything I wanted to *want* to help Dorotea, but still somehow I did not. And despite that loyalty vow she'd taken, because she knew

Abe was my brother and maybe something else as well, I darn well had to help her anyway.

She tagged along behind me as I headed down the path to the stream. We hadn't gotten far when I heard her exclaim loudly. She had stopped on the trail and was pulling off her white shoes, which suddenly were white no more. Apparently her feet had also found the donkey droppings.

Dorotea made a face at me, and she threw one shoe and then the other. The second hit my bright blue dress and left a brown smear. "Wash too!" she said.

I knew I should have nodded, picked them up, done as she asked. But the smell of them, the smell! That girl's unbelievable nerve! And the intolerable, intolerable persecution by her oppressive, domineering government!

I looked down at my dress and then at those smudged, smelly shoes. I raised my eyes to hers. And though I could have sealed my lips together, I said, "No, Dorotea. I will NOT." I was able to keep my voice quite calm until I spoke the very last word.

I saw the glow of anger get brighter in her eyes. "Yes," she said. "Rosa, you must." And she picked a little rock up out of the dirt and held it in her hand like she was fixing to pitch it at me as well.

The water in my kettle had been simmering for four days, but that rock sent the boil shooting out of the spout. I tipped the basket so the clothes fell into the dust. I picked up the left white shoe, and then the right. I went over to a thicket of fishhook-thorned cactus, and I hurled the shoes, one, two, deep into the barbed tangle.

The look on Dorotea's face turned from fury to shock. And then she started to scream at me in Spanish. Unfortunately, the only parts I understood were the naughty words she'd taught me in the buckboard on the way to El Paso.

She turned and stumbled down the path toward Pancho Villa's tent. But he'd gone somewhere overnight. She'd told me this herself. *Sorry, Dorotea,* I thought, with satisfaction. *Your papa can't fight your battles for you today.*

I put my hand in my pocket and felt for the apple I'd saved for fast Tony. Yesterday I hadn't had the gumption to steal that horse. But maybe the high-beating feeling in my chest was the thing that made gumption grow. Dorotea was so furious she'd surely make Villa's men turn me out into the desert. But I could be off on Tony before they had the chance. And then I was visited by a terrible thought. *Would getting rid of me be enough for her? Would she also take revenge on my brother?*

My stomach felt twisted tight. I could try to save Abraham, or save myself. The choice was now that simple.

I ran back to the tent and found Juanita lying on her bed. She looked deeply asleep. I grabbed Dorotea's waterskin and dumped the water from Juanita's pitcher into it. As I stuffed it in my pocket, Juanita's eyes fluttered open. Juanita was a grumpy soul, but I knew she truly cared for Dorotea. And though we had barely a word in common, I'd come to feel she cared for me too.

I took her hand. "I'm sorry," I said, and lifted her empty pitcher. She understood nothing of what I was saying, but I told her anyway. "I'll need it to cross the desert. I'm going home. But I am so deeply thankful for the kindness you've shown me." As I turned back toward the tent flap, I tripped on something and tumbled to the dirt. There was a yelp, and I saw the small brown flash of Pico scurry under Dorotea's bed.

What I had fallen on was Catalina. But not all of her.

Her flossy dark hair had vanished. There was a dome of bald white porcelain where it had been, striped with something that looked like glue. Under Dorotea's bed, Pico let out a fierce growl. He had Catalina's lovely locks clamped in his tiny, trembling jowls.

"*¡Dios mío!*" Juanita said, sitting upright.

I gave a little laugh and told the dog, "Ha! Just see what happens to you now!" I had my hand on the tent flap and was pushing it open when I heard him make a sharp bark. When I turned to look, his little snout was peeking out from beneath the bed, the doll hair hanging from it like gaudy chin whiskers. Anna Rooney would have thought him cute, and probably more than a bit pitiful. He had no idea what would befall him as soon as Dorotea saw what he'd done to her doll. The fat little thing would be set out in the desert just like Dorotea's other dog. The murdering owls would pick him off in five minutes, and the screaming canyon cat and coyote would fight over what little was left of his tiny bones. And that would be that—the complete and total and probably quite painful end of Pico the dog.

He deserved it, I thought, looking down at my ankle. And then I knew that no, he really didn't. Pico hadn't asked to be taken to the desert. Or to be dressed in clothes and made to dance for meat. He was as much a prisoner in the Villa camp as I. And he didn't deserve to die just because he didn't like it.

I knelt again beside the bed. "Darling Pico," I said in my most wheedling voice. "Give Rose the hair." Juanita pushed away her bedclothes.

His growl rose, and he shook the hair wildly, like he was killing it dead. I heard a sound of faraway shouting. I didn't have a moment to waste. I took the curls in my hand and pulled.

Pico was stronger than he looked, a fact my sore ankle already knew. The harder I tugged, the louder he growled. But finally, with a tearing sound, the hair came free.

It was matted up with dog spit, and two of the black banana curls had been chewed to the cotton scalp. I had the hair in one hand and the doll in the other when Dorotea burst through the tent flaps.

Chapter 34

Hot on Dorotea's heels were what looked like every man in Pancho Villa's army. And women too, including Audie. I saw Al push in, then Jack, and sakes alive, my brother. Everyone was there but Villa himself.

Abraham and Jack stepped forward and listened patiently to Dorotea's stream of quick-fire Spanish. She pretended to take off a shoe and pretended to throw it. But she didn't have to pretend a thing about Catalina; she just snatched the doll from my arms and left me holding her soggy hair.

Pico was circling anxiously around her feet. When Dorotea tread on his paw accidentally, he made a pitiful yip. She folded him in her arms as well, and began to cry into his fur.

Abraham looked at me with a question in his eyes, and I shook my head. And then I looked over at Pico. His eyes were bulging and his ears were skinned down on his head. He was trembling so hard he looked blurry.

I had to do it. I had to bolt the door of my mouth and lock

in the truth about who wrecked that doll. I could not let one word of it out.

At that moment Agustino came into the tent, and that caused Dorotea to relate everything she'd just said all over again.

He turned to me with fury, and when my brother shouted something at him, out came Agustino's little gun. And then he muttered words that caused two men to step forward and take hold of my arms. They pulled me out of the tent, along the path to the horse corral, and through the rocks beyond it. I heard the sounds of yelling behind me—women's voices, and men's.

I was jostled along a bit roughly, but I did not fight my captors. Getting home would take longer without the fast legs of Tony, but I had the waterskin and apple, and if I reached home before sunset, I'd have a decent chance to make it past those wild desert animals. I could still hear Abe's voice as we passed the last of the tents.

"Roooooooooooose," he cried.

It was hard, but I pushed his voice away. *Soon I'll be home*, I told myself. *Very soon.* I moved thoughts of Momma and Papa into the place in my mind where desert sun and canyon cats were crowding.

The men had chosen an awfully odd route to the open desert, climbing through the rocks, higher and higher. We passed through a jumble of small, rolling stones, and a narrow canyon decorated with pictures of men with triangle heads shooting arrows at horned deer. And then they pushed me ahead of them into a low passageway. Beyond it was a room-sized space that looked like it was the breeding spot for every scorpion in Texas. When I hesitated, one of the men gave me a hard shove and the other said, "In."

Panic pulled at my throat. "No," I said. "I won't." And so the bossier one, the one who shoved me, shoved again. I dug my fingers into the rock walls, but that man just kept pressing until I fell down. I heard the heavy clink of someone stacking rocks, and soon no more light came through the passage. They had walled me in.

My breathing was rough in my chest, and my hands were cold when I pressed them to my face. If not for Anna Rooney and her warnings about crawling scorpions, I'd have passed out right in the dirt.

So I cried instead.

There were some big rocks scattered around, and I sat down on one. And then I made myself breathe slow breaths until my lungs quit making noise. It took a long, long time, but finally I felt the crying start to ease.

And then I took account of the place that was my prison. It was a round-shaped cave room, but only part of it had a cave roof; the rest of it had tall rock walls that ended in a big slice of blue sky. Strange holes speckled the walls, some the size of a fingertip and others big enough to fit a whole fist. And then I saw some marks there too—writing and more pictures, but not crude ones like those triangle heads and deer. There was a picture of a wagon wheel and another of a boat with seven sails, some words written in a smudged charcoal black, and people's names. *A long way from Boston,* one said, and it was signed *Francis Boone, 1866*. *One Lonesome Trail—Simon Davenport, 1881*, read another.

There was a flash of movement up on the top rim of the wall. A gray-furred animal was tiptoeing along up there; it had bright, clever eyes and a black tip on its brushy tail. It paused a minute, staring down at me. And then it gave its tail a jerk, and was gone.

The writings on the rocks were everywhere. Someone had scribbled the words *My Sweetheart* and drawn a figure of a woman next to it. She had an overabundance of curves and a shortage of clothing to cover them with, and her hair flowed from her head like a waterfall. I blinked and looked again. Did she resemble Miss Polly Brunckhorst? There were words scrawled beneath her, but I would never discover what they said. As I stepped closer to read them, I heard a sound like dried beans shaking in a tin. Next to the tip of my foot, a snake head was rising from the thick coils of a large and shiny snake body.

Chapter
35

I screamed and screamed and screamed some more, and when the snake started to sway in my direction, my fingers found the holes in the rough rock and I scrambled right up the wall. When I stopped for breath, I was quite a distance from the ground.

It was the rock room's open side that I'd climbed, and up above me the furry animal had appeared again on the wall's top rim. It blinked at me, and put its head on its paws like a little dog. It looked almost charming up there, like it was waiting for me to give it a pat. I put my fingers in a big smooth hole and pulled myself up to another one. And then I did it again, and again, and again. The sky came into greater view, bright and blue above me.

I heard a sound in the distance, a rough grumble, like a deep-voiced bee. It got louder and louder, and then I saw it: the bright yellow paint of the mountain man's plane. There was another sound too—high, wild laughter.

The plane swooped toward the rocks, then bowed its

wings right and left, right and left, and the laughter turned into a shriek. Its wind blew dust into my eyes as the plane came so close I could see the white teeth of the lion on its side. Dorotea was in the seat behind Wild Bill, her hair loose around her face. She was shouting something into the wind. I saw Wild Bill shake his head, and Dorotea grasped the back of his seat and shouted again. And then the plane began to climb, higher and higher and higher. My fingers were aching, and my legs were trembling wildly, but I could no more go down than I could go up. The plane finished its rise, leveled off, and then quickly began to plunge toward the desert. Down, down, down it dropped, and the lower it went, the higher Dorotea's scream climbed. The plane was heading straight for me. I couldn't watch and I couldn't look away, but finally my eyes squeezed tight.

I wished I could have shut my ears as well when Dorotea's shriek turned into hysterical sobbing. The noise made the little animal give a yelp and scamper out of sight. I clung hard to the rock wall as the wind from the aeroplane tried to blow me free.

Finally the sound started growing fainter. When I opened my eyes, the plane was soaring off toward the horizon. Just before it flew out of sight, two small heads appeared over the edge of the back seat. One was Dorotea's and the other was Pico's. I heard her voice again. "*Shaloooooom!*" she shouted. "*Shaloooooom, Roooosaaaa!*"

◆

My legs were trembling like the tail of that snake as I inched up the wall's final stretch and heaved myself onto its top. I was greatly relieved to discover that the rim of the round rock room was nearly as wide as an El Paso boardwalk. But I was still a prisoner up there; the other side of the wall offered a mighty long drop to the canyon floor far below.

I could still see the long ribbon of that awful snake on the floor of the rock room. What would I do if that creature decided I was worth climbing for? There were small stones scattered on my ledge, and I filled my pockets with them.

And then I pulled my knees under my skirt, clasped my arms around them, and settled in for the longest hours of my life.

The sun had dropped, shadowing the canyons. Cold would arrive with the dark. I was glad for the heavy vest Dorotea had made me wear that morning, but my blue dress was less thick than my old one. As I watched the sunlight fade, it was Dorotea I was thinking of. By now she could have told everyone all she knew of Abraham and me, including the secret that would harm my brother most. And that led me to thoughts of Abraham. If not for his actions, I would have been safe and comfortable in my El Paso home. And my brother Eli was not blameless. He'd written that lying letter to our parents about Abraham helping him sell fish from his pushcart, and sent fake Abraham letters from Brooklyn too. Didn't all the problems start because he agreed to go along with Abe's lies?

But at the bottom of it all were my parents. If they'd worked harder at keeping track of Abraham and less hard at keeping too much track of me, none of this would have happened.

My legs were feeling numb and cramped, but as I tried to shift them my stone-heavy pockets nearly unbalanced me. And so I just stayed as still as I could, the press of my sadness as heavy as those rocks.

It was then that suddenly, somehow, out of nowhere, Al's voice came crowding into my head.

You're a hang-on-tight kind of girl, aren't you? he said to me, the same as he'd said in the horse corral.

"Oh, Al," I said out loud. "I think I am."

And how's that working out? the Al-in-my-head asked.

"Pretty not good at all," I replied.

Tears pushed into my eyes again, and I hung my head and let them rain freely. Why not? I'd be stuck on top of this wall until I shriveled up and died, and crying away my moisture would help hurry the process. When Abe finally came to my rescue he would find just a pile of bones.

An echoing, high-pitched squeak came from a small dark shadow that flew low over the opening of the cave room. It was a bat. Bats like to fly into your hair, Anna Rooney said, and it swooped toward me like it was aiming to, then darted away and swooped at me again. I crouched low and tried to move away from it, but those darn stones in my pockets nearly tipped me right off the wall. And then I had a very strange thought. That little flying thing was probably having itself a big belly laugh at the sight of a girl putting herself in mortal danger with the very rocks she'd gathered to keep herself safe.

The Al voice came again. *Girl, you're just afraid of everything*, it said. *Who you gonna blame for that?*

It took a long time for me to muster an answer. "Just me, I guess," I said out loud. "Just me." The feeling that followed this confession was a painful, cracking one, like something inside me had been hammered in two. And then all the truths I'd been holding off from myself rolled over me in a suffocating wave. I had snooped. I had threatened to tattle. And I had named my brother a liar when it turned out I was just as big a liar myself.

The truth wave hurt, but instead of crying again, I reached into my pocket and pulled out a stone. And then I named it Dorotea, and tossed it hard away from me. I tossed another and another, calling out the names of Momma and Papa, Anna Rooney, Eli, and finally Abe. And then I turned out both pockets and watched all the rest of the blame I was carrying bounce and tumble to the faraway ground.

Chapter 36

Unfortunately, the waterskin and apple fell with the stones. I was quite sure I was too hungry and cold to drop into sleep, and the snoring sound that revealed someone was guarding the rock room entrance didn't help. But I must have dozed off in spite of it all, because I startled in the middle of the night to the sound of a horse call and the ring of hoof on rock.

Soon after came gunfire. It was three shots—bang, bang, bang, followed by an awful, echoing cry. *If he is lucky,* Dorotea had said, *they will kill him fast.* There was small comfort that there had been just one cry, not two. But for all I knew, Abraham was imprisoned now as well.

I was awake a long time, but I somehow dozed off again. And then a noise of clinking rock jolted me awake once more.

The moon was still shining brightly, but from my high, rocky perch, I could see the desert's edge held the soft light of very early morning. I heard the sound of footsteps, and at the moment I realized what a fine rifle target I made on the ledge, Juanita appeared in the cave below me. I was so very, very glad to see her.

She was carrying a bundle under her arm, and she put it down and looked around the cave room, then looked around again. When her eyes finally found me on the rim above, her mouth creased into the widest grin I'd seen her face wear. She picked up the bundle and tossed it up toward me. It struck the wall and fell back down, so she picked it up and tried again. It took her two more tries to make it land on the ledge beside me.

The bundle was a rolled-up sombrero. It was quite a thoughtful gift to bring, as I'd left my bonnet in the tent, and my skin wasn't the kind that fared well in bright sunshine. Inside of it were a hunk of cheese and a small book, the kind called a dime novel. I didn't have much fondness for reading them, but I knew I'd seen this particular one before. And then I remembered where. The pair of hard-riding cowboys on its cover had also graced the book Shmuley had patted so tenderly in my family's parlor.

There was a likeness of the author printed on the back, and it gave me quite a start to realize she looked familiar too. Her hair was long and it waved on her shoulders, and her face looked less hard-bitten, but it bore a great resemblance to the one worn by Audie's brother Al. There were words beneath the picture, and the moon offered just enough light to make them out:

What follows is a fair and true revelation of how my sister Audrelia Muggs and I became a pair of

infamous stagecoach robbers, cattle thieves, card
sharks, and murderers. We started as orphans and
ended up bandits, and lived to tell the tale.

I opened the book and found bold pencil writing on the
first page. Reading it made me gasp right out loud.

To Rose, it said, *who is much more adventurous than*
she thinks she is, and who will also live to tell her tale. It
was signed *Alice Muggs*.

The snoring coming from the passage stuttered and then
resumed. Juanita frowned at the noise. "*La ruta de escape está*
ahí," she said, and pointed at the ledge I was sitting on. She
pointed again and nodded encouragingly, and I nodded back.
She was telling me something of importance, that was clear.
How I wished I'd *ever* thought to learn that Spanish language.

And then she said, "*Adios, Rosa. Viajes seguros!*" and
with that, Juanita left the way she'd come in. I believe it was
the very first time she'd used my name.

I read the book's inscription again. I read it three times
more, and then I laughed out loud. Tough-talking, fast-
riding, pants-wearing Al was a *woman*? I opened it to see
if it held more information, and found additional writing
scribbled on its blank first page. It was in my brother's hand!

Dear Rose,

I am sorry they have put you in the round rock room as
a punishment for defying Dorotea, but I have been assured
no harm will come to you!

More good news: I have been named a lieutenant in Villa's army, which is an important honor, and a comforting one. Today, you shall accompany Dorotea to Mexico. Your presence will keep her happy, and this will allow Villa to focus on a very important battle. And afterward, I have gained his permission to return you to our parents and your safe and simple childhood world. Yes, Rose, I finally told him the truth—that we are sister and brother—and all is well.

Please don't worry.

Your loving brother,
Abraham

Abe had circled the word "truth" with a heavy black line.

It was clear that telling me of this promotion was Abraham's way of saying Dorotea had not told Villa he had been a spy. But his note also informed me of something else that deep inside I already knew: Abraham cared more for the freedom of strangers than he did for his sister. For my brother, saving one person would never, ever be as important as saving the world.

I set down the book, but I accidentally placed it too close to the outer side of the ledge and it tipped off, falling toward the boulder field below. But it hit quickly with a loud smack, and when I peered over the side, I saw it had landed on another ledge. It was a ledge of good size, and only a body's length or so below me. To the right of it was a steep drop, and to the left were large, crushing rocks. But below it was yet another ledge, and under *that* seemed to be some kind of rough trail of rubble that wound toward the canyon floor. A person could possibly hang from those ledges with their hands and drop down, praying hard they didn't hit too far left or right. And then, perhaps, the trail could be followed and the horse corral found, where a smooth-gaited brown horse could offer a ride across the desert.

I appraised the edge of my own rock ledge, then glanced at the ends of my sleeves just to double-check. Yes, there they were, both hands. *See that?* I said to the Al-in-my-head. *Found them.*

I tied the sombrero strings around my neck, and when I put the cheese into my pocket I felt hard metal in the pocket's lining. The tiny hands Dorotea had given me had wedged there and survived the flinging of the stones. *Milagros*, she'd called them—miracles. I'd certainly need every kind of miracle to do what I had to do next.

My fingers were not trembling, but they were a bit clammy. I wiped them on my dress, then lay down flat and moved my feet to the edge, and then over it. At the edge I found rough bits of rock that made holds for my hands, and worked my feet on the wall for footing, but without success. Below me, the ledge that had looked so welcoming now seemed ridiculously far away. But it was too late—there was absolutely no way I could climb back up.

And so I dangled there, the rock biting hard into my fingers. There was clearly just one thing to do, and that was to cling there a little bit longer than I could stand.

"Okay," I finally told myself. "Let go now!"

My willful hands refused to listen. I tried again. "One, two, three!" I said, but my fingers held on stubborn-tight.

The muscles of my arms were paining me, and my legs had begun to quake. Finally, out of nowhere, I heard Audie's voice as clearly as if she were hanging on the ledge beside me. *Let go, gal!* she told me. She was joined by the voice of someone who was not Audie's brother, but her sister, and was speaking the words she'd said in the horse corral with so much scorn.

You waiting on somebody to pry your fingers loose for you?

I fell like a stone.

Chapter 37

I landed hard on my dog-bit ankle, but the pain felt far away, like it belonged to someone else. I lay there a while, breathing hard, and then I sat up and put Al's book into my pocket.

The drop to the next ledge felt as easy as falling from the back of a horse to the ground.

The trail I found at the bottom of the cliff took me high above the place where the soldiers' tents were staked. I could hear no sounds of stirring from there. It was still very early morning. I thanked my luck that Villa's army was a group of late sleepers.

As the trail wound downward, I smelled a scent of horses. As I felt my pocket for the apple that was no longer there, I smelled a scent of men. The corral came into view, and a dreadful second later, so did soldiers. They were swarming everywhere, strapping saddles onto horses, working bridles onto their heads. My heart dropped into my feet and then plunged past them, heading somewhere into the deep center of the earth.

I ducked low behind a boulder to avoid being seen. How would I escape now? I had absolutely no idea.

Not far from me, two horses stood saddled and waiting. The black one snaked its head around to bite the white horse next to it, and that creature whirled and kicked, jerking free from the man holding its reins. It kicked out one more time, and galloped up the path toward me. "*¡Bruja!*" the man shouted with anger. But he didn't come after it.

The horse was Blanca. It was no surprise that even the other horses couldn't stand her. Blanca was no Tony, but at least she was a horse. And she was also a horse I would not have to saddle.

She came to a stop in front of me and snorted, and then she nosed the pocket the cheese was in. I grabbed the ends of her reins and pulled her quickly down the trail. Once we were out of view from the corral, I stood on a rock, hoisted my skirt, and put one leg over her back. It took three more tries and a mighty scramble to mount Blanca, but finally I was sitting on top of her.

The trail took us into the narrow rock passage I'd gone through that first day. When we came out into the open desert, I could hear horses calling from behind me, and the sound of men's voices. But ahead, the sun's first rays were touching the mountains that sliced through El Paso. I turned Blanca toward them.

I felt a tingling sensation brush up and down my arms. It could have been fear, but I think it was excitement. I was leaving the Villa camp and I wasn't heading for battle. I was leaving the Villa camp and I was going home!

I thumped at Blanca with my legs to help her find her jolting gait, but she kept her plodding walk. I pulled my legs from her side and kicked hard at her belly, but she didn't find my heels a cause to quicken. I took the end of the reins, and just as I'd seen Dorotea do, whipped them a quick one-two on both sides of her neck. Her skin shuddered as if a fly had landed, but her feet kept shuffling.

We'd been moving at this plodding pace for what seemed like forever when I heard a terrible trembling roar coming from the sky. When I looked up, I saw the most amazing sight: not one, but three bright-winged planes were flying there. And then I heard a loud whirring sound from somewhere behind us. A shiny black motorcar was approaching, and it was moving far faster than Blanca. If Al, one of Villa's best riders, couldn't get her to move, what chance did I have? I kicked her again and Blanca thrashed her tail and stopped altogether.

I had a wild urge to jump off the horse and run, but the flat, bare landscape didn't offer a single place to hide.

The motorcar drew closer. It had a brass-bound trunk tied to its roof, and the *campesino* named Felipe was at the wheel. Behind him was Juanita, and I felt my teeth come together hard at the sight of Dorotea sitting right next to her.

She was leaning out the open window, holding Pico so his paws flopped over the window's edge. When they drew close, she smiled a wide, happy smile. "*Hola*, Rosa!" she called. "Blanca is the most stubborn of horses, is she not?"

She said something to Felipe, and the automobile came to a halt beside us.

"Rosa," she said, "I know you won't want to miss a fine, fine battle."

If she ordered Felipe to drag me into the automobile, I couldn't stop her, but what I could still do was plead with the truth.

"Dorotea," I said, "I am not an orphan. I have a mother and a father in El Paso, and I'm going to go home to them. I'm going home to my family."

She didn't answer, just lifted Pico up in the air and dangled him out of the car window. She held him there a moment, swaying him back and forth. "I should just drop him here, no?" she said. "He is not a good dog." And then she pulled him back into the car and covered the top of his furry round head with loud, wet kisses. All I could see of him were the tips of his trembling ears.

"*Tío* says he will buy me a much better doll when we come again to El Paso. He also says it is a very brave kind of girl who climbs out of the round room, the kind of girl who could help the Revolution." Juanita moved closer to her on the seat, her lean face half lit by the rays of the rising sun. Dorotea looked at her and sighed. "But *Tío* says you must let a person be who they are—even if being someone else would be good for a whole nation." Again, her face was his face—her eyes, touched by the morning sunshine, the exact same glint of yellow-brown. "It is the *libertad* you seek, yes?" she said. "Like our Jewish Moses fellow who also traveled a desert."

Juanita moved her eyebrows up and down, up and down. She was smiling. She put her hand on Dorotea's arm.

"I am bossy, Juanita tells me, but I must say to you this," Dorotea said. "If you want to get to El Paso before nighttime, you better go a little faster." She spoke to Felipe again, and the car backed, then moved forward again, stopping just inches from Blanca's side. Dorotea leaned so far out of the window she was in danger of toppling, and then *smack!* She hit Blanca's hindparts with the flat of both hands.

I made a small scream as the horse lurched into the horrible gait that had carried me to the Villa camp five days before. I grabbed the saddle horn and held it tight. But I did apologize for this to the Al-in-my-head.

"*You may keep my mother's vest,*" Dorotea shouted as the car started moving. "*It will make you think of me. But I will see you again, my friend!*" I could still hear her laughter as the car turned south toward Mexico and chugged from my sight.

◆

Once Blanca was moving, I couldn't get her to stop, even when it seemed like my insides were jiggling right out of me. We hadn't traveled long in this painful way when I heard another sound coming from behind me; a low, rumbling roar that seemed to shake the dry earth. It grew louder and louder, and when I turned my head to glance back, I saw an enormous cloud of dust with horse legs churning below. The entirety of Pancho Villa's army was galloping behind me and Blanca, fixing to flatten us like a mouse under the wheels of a stagecoach. "You must let a person be who they are," Villa had told Dorotea. But more than once, I had seen him change his mind.

I tried to steer the horse off left, then right, but she wasn't much in the mood to take direction. And then suddenly, a miracle: her back arched beneath me, and her legs began working faster, and just like that we were flying. The wind banged the hat against my back, and pulled the ribbons right off the ends of my braids. As I felt the sombrero fall away, my hair came loose and whipped crazily into my mouth and my eyes. I could barely see a thing.

Quickly the noise of the army grew more distant. "*Go, girl, go!*" I shouted. Blanca's breath racheted in her lungs, and we ate up that desert land like it was sweet honey and apples.

But then it all returned again: the roar, the thunder, the yells. And though Blanca was running her heart out, her heart couldn't make her run quite fast enough. The noise grew louder, and then it was deafening and the army was all around us.

I saw the yellow-serape man Jack had interviewed on my left, and Agustino flying by on my right. And hot on his heels galloped a beautiful black horse bearing *General* Pancho Villa himself.

He passed us easily, then reined in the horse so that it drew even with Blanca. He looked right at me, his eyes burning like coals from a fire. And then he turned his face ahead and yelled, "*¡Luchamos por la libertad! ¡Viva la revolución!*" He raised his whip in the air and brought it down on his horse's side, and they were gone.

Two more riders appeared. They were Audie and Al. Audie grinned at me and shook her pointing finger at the saddle horn I clutched, but Al just waved the nose of a long rifle in the air. *"Whoo hoo, Rose girl!"* Al yelled. *"Whoo hoooooo!"*

Behind them, all in a cluster, rode the women I'd seen fixing meals and washing. To my everlasting surprise, every single one of them was draped in bullet belts and carrying a rifle. It would take a mighty passion for freedom to do all that housekeeping work and then strap on a gun and go shooting in a battle as well. I hoped Jack Reed had taken down their stories too.

A two-horse rig pulling a cannon rumbled by next, and then a smiling Don Hicks and Tony. In their dust cloud galloped Jack Reed and my brother Abraham. Jack yelled something at me I couldn't decipher, and Abraham drew so close we were nearly rubbing stirrups. His words came to me quite distinctly. *"Viva, Rose!"* he shouted. *"This is a far better plan than any I could have imagined!"* And he let his horse fly past.

He could not possibly hear my reply, but I made it anyway. *"I love you, Abraham!"* I screamed into the wind. *"And please do not get yourself killed!"*

Chapter 38

The riders followed the same route as Dorotea's motorcar, heading toward Mexico. In the time it takes to count to ten, Villa's entire army became a receding cloud of dirt. And in the time it takes to count to twenty-five, they were a far-off ball of kicked-up sand.

Blanca's strides grew slower, and pretty soon she'd returned to the speed of a Sunday stroll. We ambled toward El Paso for a while at this easy pace—both of us, I think, happy to get our breath back. My thoughts turned to the hot bath waiting for me at the end of this day, and the comfort of my very own bed. But just when I was beginning to wonder how I'd ever tell my parents about Abraham, I spied yet another ball of dust ahead of us. And then Blanca saw it too, and though I yanked the reins as hard as I could, somehow the old thing managed it all again—the churning legs, the roaring breath—and all my strength couldn't stop her. "*No, no, no!*" I screamed, but onward she raced, straight toward that unknown cloud.

I made out two men on horses first, one in black clothes and the other with flying hair and a cowboy hat. Behind them was a box wagon pulled by a team, which was followed by several more men astride.

The men in front seemed to slow when they saw me. They shouted something.

It sounded like...my name!

Blanca was pulling so hard, she nearly ran us right into the wagon. But the man who leaped from the wagon seat and grabbed Blanca's bridle was Papa. And Momma and Miss Polly were in the wagon too!

Papa pulled me down from the saddle, and he and Momma pressed on each side of me so close I could barely breathe. Miss Polly stood next to us with tears running down her face. I clutched at my parents as hard as they clutched at me, but finally I pulled free. "How did this happen?" I said. "How did you know?"

Papa was crying too. "We went to the sheriff, Rose, the very day you disappeared into thin air. They told us they knew nothing and could do nothing. We asked everyone we knew if they'd seen you that morning, and your mother was determined to knock on every single door in town. But the next day we saw a dark-haired young women in a wagon speeding out of town, and—"

My mother interrupted him. "I knew it was you! He said it could not be. But there are things a mother knows!"

"Your teacher, Miss Polly, came to us then, with that young man over there," Papa continued, and pointed to the long-haired rider, who turned out to be Thurman. The second rider was Shmuley. He looked about as happy as a person could be, and if he'd known about the book in my pocket, he would have looked even happier. "Together we made a rescue plan," Papa said. "The wagon was for you to ride on, Rose, and your mother and Miss Polly—well, they insisted to come."

He started to chuckle, and then to laugh. The happier Papa gets, the louder his voice becomes, and the sound of his laughter boomed like rifle shots across the flat desert land. But then his laughter turned to sobs.

"We come to rescue my only daughter, the little girl I have spent my life protecting. But what do we find?" he said, wiping his sleeve at the tears on his cheeks. "We find she has no need because she is rescuing herself!"

Shmuley's hands began making a jerky path from his blue neckerchief to his hat brim and back. Thurman took his hat off and looked hard at the ground. He glanced up and our eyes met. *I'm sorry*, his eyes said, and then he directed them down again, but not before I noted they were a startlingly nice shade of blue.

Momma reached over to hug me again, but her dress tangled in a creosote bush. As she bent to unhook it, she exclaimed, "What is this?" When she straightened, she had a square of something white clutched in her hand. She brought it close to her face.

"It is a letter," she said, her voice trembling, "and it is addressed to the name of Abraham Solomon!" I couldn't believe my eyes. She'd found the very piece of paper that had started all my trouble.

Papa bent over and snatched something from the ground too. The color of the envelope he held up was pink, and when Miss Polly caught sight of it she turned that shade as well.

I rode toward El Paso with Thurman on my left side, Shmuley on my right. Blanca had quit her prancing and gone back to imitating a plow horse, but she fancied up her pace a bit as we reached town. When we turned onto Chapparal Street, I spotted the tall black hat of Rabbi Zeilonka. He was crossing the road, and as we approached, a herd of sheep came swarming around a corner. There was a farmer behind them on a horse, but the creatures seemed to be running out of control.

Rabbi Zeilonka saw them, but not in time. *Baa*-ing and bleating, they set on him like a woolly flood. I gasped as an especially big one pushed straight between his legs. He swayed wildly, and then landed smack on the sheep's broad back. He clung there laughing as it galloped him along through the dust. And that is how I came to know that there is nothing at all on this whole earth that is completely absurd or impossible.

Finally we drew near my home. Three girls were walking on the road ahead of us. Thurman touched his hat solemnly as we passed, and Shmuley pulled at his bandanna. One of the girls was Anna Rooney, and it gave me more than a little pleasure to note that when she recognized me, she traded her tight-lipped look of I-know-everything for a slack-mouthed I-know-absolutely-nothing-at-all.

Chapter 39

The lights winked off and the screen started to glow as the projector cast a shifting beam upon it. Twisting curls of tobacco smoke rose from the seats in front of us, and a newsreel began to play. First came a story on the new, round Zeppelin airships from Germany; then one on England's king, a man with a great long face like someone's old hunting hound. None of it interested Momma and me. It was the main feature we'd come for, a cowboy thriller with a man named Tom Mix and his amazing trick horse Tony, but we had to get through all the newsreels first.

I'd spied the lobby card for the movie in the theater window the previous week, and it had given me a jolt—the name of the cowboy, "Tom Mix," sounded awfully similar to that of Don Hicks, the rope-trick fellow in the camp of Pancho Villa. And was it a coincidence that their shiny brown horses were called the same name? Before my time in that place, I might have made a mistake and said yes.

As the newsreel played on, I noticed a foul scent rising up from my calfskin shoes. Momma would scold me if she knew I'd worn them to clean Blanca's stall, so I pushed my feet as far under the seat as they'd go.

Momma and Papa and I had come to an important agreement after I'd returned. We decided I would try things like silky hair ribbons, pretty shoes, and stitchery if in return they'd be willing to try having a daughter who sang in public, rode a horse, and wasn't lectured about marriage.

Blanca had lost some of her crankiness since she'd taken residence in the stable behind our house, and using a horse-drawn wagon for his meat deliveries instead of a handcart was making Papa's life much easier. When she wasn't occupied with Papa, I took her out myself for rides. She pulled a wagon far more willingly than she bore a rider, but still I believed she was enjoying our daily ramblings around town as much as I was.

I never strayed far from familiar streets in case Villa decided to send someone to steal his favorite horse back, though part of me hoped he would—and that someone would be Abraham. There had been just one small article published in the newspaper about the battle Villa's army had fought on the day I escaped. Much blood had been shed on all sides, the article said, and the *bandidos* had retreated into Mexico. Not a single letter from Abraham had made it to me or Miss Polly since.

And I wasn't the only one thinking about Abraham.

Word had gotten around El Paso of his adventures, and suddenly all sorts of folks had all kinds of things to say about him. It didn't surprise me that Mr. Pickens labeled Abe a darn fool, but Rabbi Zeilonka's voice cracked with passion as he talked about his "noble sacrifice for the liberation of those less fortunate." If someone had cared to ask my thoughts on the subject, I might have admitted I agreed with him.

The Rose who had not yet lived in a *bandido* camp would have never understood this. The Rose before the *bandido* camp would not have understood a lot of things.

In that place I'd been a child's slave and a helpless sister, felt fearful and suspicious of others, and caused others to feel fearful and suspicious of me. I'd met soldiers and barnstormers, and women who acted free as men, fallen from a horse by accident and a high rock on purpose. I'd learned that my brother and I were both of us bald-faced liars, and that I couldn't save someone who didn't want saving. I'd done all that and lived, and now there seemed only one thing left to be afraid of, and that was an echoing gunshot followed by a horrible, horrible cry.

But Abraham had to be Abraham, no matter where it led him, no matter what anyone thought of his ways, and no matter whose heart broke from loving him. Just as I had to be Rose, the kind of person I was, not the kind of person anyone else would have me be.

My friend Gabriela had begun teaching me Spanish. I was, she said, "*ni aquí, ni allá,*" which she told me meant in between worlds, neither here nor there. Ever since I'd returned from the camp of Pancho Villa, this was exactly how I felt. I'd bet my brother Abraham would say it described him as well.

But this was not something I thought Momma would easily understand. It had taken nearly every bit of these last weeks to settle her after she'd read that letter to Abe that she pulled from the creosote bush, though she did take the pink-envelope letter a great deal better than both I and Miss Polly had expected. And though she finally managed not to cry every single time someone spoke to her of Abe, soon most everyone knew not to.

She knew he had gone to a battle and could have been killed, and I wasn't about to tell her that even if he survived it, within the Villa camp an even more horrible fate could have befallen him.

◆

The third newsreel began with a view of horse cavalry fording a river and swarming across a desert landscape. And then a line of words appeared beneath it that read MEXICAN FIGHTERS REGROUP AFTER CRUSHING DEFEAT. My face prickled with a flush of sudden heat. My mother pushed back against her seat.

An image of shabbily dressed men standing in a line flashed onto the screen. And yes, yes, it was them, the *bandidos*, Pancho Villa prominent at their center. But his hard-boiled eyes were aimed softly at a small, pretty girl with a leg brace who stood in front of the soldiers, holding up a flower for her father to smell.

Agustino was on his left and Felipe was to his right, along with two of his guards. I recognized Wild Bill and Farnum T. Fish among the Villistas behind them, and the Misses Alice and Audrelia, who scowled so fiercely, if you didn't know better you'd surely have thought them both men. I scanned all the faces quickly, and then I did it again.

But no.

My brother was not among them.

◆

And then a horse galloped into the right side of the scene. It reared up and paddled the air with its forelegs. When the rider took off his hat and waved it, his forehead was stained with a wide mark.

I turned to my mother when I heard her give a gasp. She was looking up at the screen with big, staring eyes.

I took hold of her arm. "Momma," I said. She didn't seem to hear me. Slowly she pushed to her feet.

"Momma?" I said, giving her arm a tap. "*Momma?*"

She shook me off, lifted her trembling hand, and pointed it toward the flickering images.

"THAT'S HIM!" she pronounced, in a voice so loud not even the man running the clicking projector could have missed it. "THAT'S MY BOY ABIE UP THERE!" And her smile was so bright with pride it could have cleared off every trace of darkness from an outlaw's heart.

Author's Note

Although this book is a work of fiction, it was inspired by real events and historical figures.

The Mexican Revolution began in 1910 with a people's uprising against the dictator-like rule of Mexican President Porfirio Díaz. At that time in Mexico, the ruling class, which included Díaz, was comprised of wealthy aristocrats—many of them descended from Spanish colonists.

Meanwhile, with Díaz as president, the poor had little hope of improving their lives and little or no opportunity to legally own land. Great sources for reading and understanding this history better are *Pancho Villa* by Alicia Alarcon Armendá (Selector, 2010), *Pancho Villa: Rebel of the Mexican Revolution* by Mary Englar (Capstone Press, 2006), John Reed's *Insurgent Mexico* (Red and Black Publishers, 2009), and *The Wild Chihuahuas of Mexico* by Traude Gomez Rhine (Tampico Press Books, 2014).

The Revolution had several factions and leaders, including Pancho Villa, a folk hero who, as a saying of that time proclaimed, was "hated by thousands and loved by millions," and commanded a citizen army called the Villistas. Villa was born June 5, 1878, in La Coyotada, San Juan del Río, Durango, Mexico. He went by several names, but his real one was Doroteo Arango Arámbula, and he was the eldest son of poor farmworkers. He worked the land too, as a child, and had no schooling after age seven; he was ashamed of his illiteracy when he grew up.

Stories of Villa's past differ, but he became an outlaw when he either shot at or killed the landowner's son for attacking his sister. As a leader, he was known for helping the poor and was also notorious for his brutal treatment of anyone he deemed an enemy.

The Villistas' revolutionary cause attracted sympathizers such as famed journalist John Reed, who actually spent four months living with the Villa gang and writing stories about them for *Metropolitan Magazine* and other publications; famous movie cowboy Tom Mix; and an assortment of well-known barnstormers such as Farnum T. Fish, Mickey McQuire, and Wild Bill Heath. Even the legendary bank robber Butch Cassidy is said to have gotten involved with the Villistas as an instructor in the art of blowing up trains. Though they were not with the Villa gang at the same time, I chose to place these characters there for the purposes of this fictional story.

Rose and Abraham, too, were real people, and distant relatives of mine. I based them in El Paso, Texas, instead of San Antonio, their actual hometown. My father's father, their first cousin, claimed to have been born in San Antonio but his family moved to Indiana and then Brooklyn, New York. I have childhood memories of colorful serapes and broad sombreros that decorated a bedroom in my great-aunt's house in Bensonhurst, Brooklyn, and my family has long told intriguing stories of the Texas relatives who would visit their eastern cousins. Rose brought my great-aunt gifts of Mexican clothing, and Abe, who would arrive wearing a cowboy hat and sharp-toed boots, liked to pretend he was a bumbling hick at the local billiard hall, so he could pool-shark everyone in sight.

The final chapter in the book, in which Rose and Momma discover Abraham onscreen, was inspired by an actual event. In the early 1930s my father, who was a very young boy at the time, was sitting in a theater with his grandmother, Abraham's father's sister. When a newsreel about Pancho Villa came on, she stood up and proclaimed to the audience, "That's my Abie on the screen!"

By the time the Mexican Revolution finally ended, more than nine hundred thousand people had lost their lives. The Díaz government was replaced by a series of power-hungry leaders, and eventually Álvaro Obregón, who had been commander in chief of the Mexican army, was elected president. Like Díaz, Obregón loved power, but fortunately he loved peace as well, and he accepted many of the revolutionaries' demands. The war ended officially in 1917, with the creation of the Constitution of Mexico, but it took many more years for the fighting to stop completely. In 1923 Pancho Villa was assassinated, probably by decree of President Obregón. His final words are said to have been: "Don't let it end like this. Tell them I said something." His name and his legend, immortalized in the song "La Cucaracha," live on in Mexican and American folklore.

Though my family doesn't know what ultimately became of Abraham, an article that my sister found from the March 9, 1932, edition of *The Light*, a San Antonio-based newspaper (see pages 230-231), offers clues about the rest of his life. After the Mexican Revolution ended, he fought bandits in Panama as a soldier for hire, and he owned a cattle ranch in Colorado and, later, a South Seas pearl-fishing fleet. After he weathered a bandit raid on a plantation he owned in an undisclosed tropical location, he spent a year in jail—and then his trail vanishes. The article said lawyers were hunting for him so he could sign papers related to a lawsuit, but family legend says they were looking for him so that the American government could give him the money he had earned for the time he spent spying on Pancho Villa.

Rose married, raised children, and ended up living in California. But another family legend says she also became a singer and had something to do with the popular spread of the song "La Cucaracha."

Further Notes

Agustino
The character of Agustino was inspired by Rudolfo Fiero, Pancho Villa's real-life right-hand man. A ruthless soldier who was nicknamed "the butcher," he died in 1920 when he accidentally stepped in quicksand and his men decided not to save him.

Rabbi Zeilonka
The character of Rabbi Zeilonka was inspired by Rabbi Martin Zeilonka, a German native who came to El Paso in 1900. He is said to have been a strict disciplinarian who looked down on the bad behavior that frequently went on in the town, and helped form a committee to regulate gambling parlors and saloons. His son was also a rabbi, but his grandson was a dentist—and coincidentally, for part of my childhood was my family's dentist.

Jews in Russia at the Turn of the Nineteenth Century
Before 1900, the countries of Russia and Poland held the largest Jewish population in the world. Unfortunately, these populations were heavily persecuted, forced to live in restricted areas, and forbidden to work at certain kinds

of jobs. Jewish men were often conscripted into the army for repeated terms of service, which was what happened to the fictional Rose's father. Additionally, there were frequent violent attacks called pogroms on Jewish settlements that were secretly government supported. It's no small wonder that as the prospects for creating a life of unlimited possibility in the free, wide-open spaces of America increased, many Jewish families immigrated. Between 1880 and 1920, more than two million Eastern European Jews came to live in America.

The Mud Golem of Prague

The golem Rose references in her attempt to flee from the livery is a legendary mud creature that can be made to perform any task. Legend has it that as a way to protect Jewish people from anti-Semitic attacks in the town of Prague, Czechoslovakia, in the sixteenth century, the chief rabbi of Prague, Judah Loew ben Bezalel, created a golem and brought it to life by writing *emet*, the Hebrew word for "truth," on its forehead. Large and manlike in form, golems were similar to Frankenstein's monster—they would do what they were told but could easily get out of control—and the rabbi's golem quickly became very violent. Rabbi Loew ended the golem's reign by erasing one letter of the word written on its head—which turned it into *met*, the Hebrew word for "dead."

The Czar's Jeweled Eggs

The eggs Papa mentions in Pickens's store are the ornate, elaborately bejeweled eggs that were given by the Russian Czar Alexander III to his wife as Easter presents. After Alexander's death, the eggs were presented annually by his son, Czar Nicholas II, to his own wife.

Jewish Immigration to the American West

It's not a widely known fact, but in the early 1900s many Jewish people immigrated to the United States via the port of Galveston, Texas. In 1907 a wealthy Jewish New Yorker named Jacob Schiff decided he needed to do something about the dangerous overcrowding in many East Coast cities that was being caused by Jewish and Eastern European immigration. He developed an immigration assistance program called the Galveston Plan, which recruited Jewish immigrants to populate America's western region. Between 1907 and 1914, ten thousand Jewish immigrants came to the U.S. through Galveston.

Villa's Desert Hideaway

The secret Villa gang hideout in this story was inspired by a real-life geographical landmark called Hueco Tanks, which lies in the desert just east of El Paso. Known for its remarkable jumbled rock formations and extensive Native American pictographs, Hueco Tanks is a natural oasis that has sheltered humans for thousands of years. This is largely because of the availability of water there; the word *hueco* refers to the natural hollows and pockets that form in the rock, collecting and holding precious water. Once a private ranch, Hueco Tanks is now a Texas state park anyone can visit. More information can be found at www.texasbeyondhistory.net/hueco/

Spanish Glossary

Animado: Animated

Bruja: Witch

Caliente: Hot

Dios mío: Oh my God

El Paso: A shortening of the Spanish name *El paso del río del norte*, which means "the crossing of the river to the north"

Frijoles: Beans

La ruta de escape está ahí: The escape route is right there

Loco: Crazy

¡Luchamos por la libertad! ¡Viva la revolución!: We fight for liberty! Long live the Revolution!

Macuche: A tobacco-like plant

Milagro: Miracle [*Milagro(s)* is also the name for tiny religious charms used for centuries in Latin America to ask saints and religious figures for support and guidance.]

Mi niña bonita: My pretty girl

¿Qué ocurre?: What is it?

Tío: Uncle

Viajes seguros: Safe travel

Yiddish Glossary

Challah: A loaf of braided egg bread

Haroses: A sweet condiment made from fruit and nuts that is served at a Passover dinner. It is said to represent the mortar used to build the Pharaoh's pyramids.

Kreplach: Small filled dumplings usually served in soup

Naches: Pride

Seder: A ceremonial dinner that marks the start of the Jewish holiday of Passover

Shayna: Beautiful or Pretty

Additional Terms

Baruch hata adonai, elohanu melech ha'olum, boray poree hagofen [Hebrew, phonetic spelling]: Blessed are you, the Lord our God, ruler of the universe, creator of the fruit of the vine.

Cantor: The Latin word for singer. It is often used to refer to someone who sings worshipful songs during religious ceremonies.

CROCKETT 4040
FOR THE LIGHT
If your paper fails to arrive on time or if
you want it daily or Sunday.

THE SAN ANTONIO LIGHT

AN INDEPENDENT TEXAS NEWSPAPER

SECTION B
GENERAL NEWS
Profit thru a real estate investment.
See Light Classified Ads

VOL. LII—NO. 51.　　　SAN ANTONIO, TEXAS, WEDNESDAY, MARCH 9, 1932.　　　VOL. LII—NO. 51.

DIPLOMAT FROM RUMANIA VISITS S.A.

Dimanesco Goes to Mexico to Study Agrarian Reform Plan.

NEW QUESTIONS IN AIRPLANE CONTEST

Light Presents Two More Free Air Trip Problems.

Roy Bean--'The Law West of the Pecos'

One of the Oft-Told Tales, Including Oratory of Famed Jurist as He Sentenced Mexican to Death, Is Told By Everett Lloyd in His Book of Legends

Dead Man Is Fined When Bean Finds Money in His Pocket.

SUIT TO HALT SCHOOL BOARD CONTRACT IS DISMISSED

Court Dissolves Injunction Staying Signing of Agreement.

Pleas Changed in S.A. Liquor Cases

5 Are Accepted by Literary Club

Airplane Contest Rules

S. A. Has Part in Eagle Pass Fete

Nurses Will Fly to S. A. Meet

Army Takes a Man on Vehicle

SHERIFF WILL EXAMINE PAIR

ELLA CINDERS—The Wheels Move

Mrs. Uhr in Pen to Begin Life Term for Mate's Murder

GARNER BODY TO MEET HERE

Phones in Service Decrease 50,330, Company Reports

Poverty Plea of 2 in Liquor Trials

Detectives Find Stolen Overcoat; No Arrest Made

History Classes Choose Officers

TEXAS HISTORY MOVIES—The Texans Complete...

REMEMBER THE ALAMO!　REMEMBER GOLIAD!

Engineer Troop School Postponed

Texas Rabbis to Hold S. A. Confab

Appended to Spring Skirts

$50 Fine Is Paid in Auto Fatality

Will Rogers Says

BEVERLY HILLS, Calif.

WILL ROGERS.

Every once in a while you come across a life story that, in its color and action, seems almost fictional. Such a life is that of a San Antonio native son, Abraham Solomon.

A typical soldier of fortune, he has wandered all over the face of the globe in his 38 years, has fought under many flags, and is probably right now mixed up some way in the Sino - Japanese trouble, his folks believe.

No matter where war breaks out, Solomon usually turns up in a short time. He fought with Pancho Villa in Mexico and he fought against bandits in Panama.

A few years ago he decided to settle down and bought a large ranch in Colorado. After a successful year he concluded he wasn't made for such a quiet life. He next bobbed up in the South Seas as half-owner of a pearl fishing fleet.

His family next heard of him as a plantation owner in a tropical country. There was a bandit raid on the plantation and trouble followed, with Solomon landing in jail for a year. He survived a devastating fever and the year in jail, and on his return to the United States, brought suit for $60,000.

His attorney in Washington and his people here are now looking for the wanderer. It seems that something has to be signed before the case can go any further. They have advertised in papers everywhere, but have received no word of him.

So it looks like they'll just have to wait until he bobs up, maybe four or five years from now, goodness knows where or how.

(This page and previous) Front page of *The San Antonio Light* with column 1 detail of "Around the Plaza" by Jeff Davis, March 9, 1932 © *San Antonio Express News*/Zuma.

Image courtesy of Ancestry.com.

Acknowledgments

Creating this book has sometimes felt like a long ride across a desert landscape.
I owe so many people a huge debt of gratitude for keeping me from tumbling out of the saddle.

Many thanks to a long, talented conga line of writer's groupies, including Pat Richards, Agnes Dietrich, Pat O'Connor, Stephanie McElrath, and Tiffany Lydecker for listening to early pages and sitting patiently while I droned on about the Mexican Revolution; to Carol Shank and Gina Tucci for in-progress critiques and a deep and ongoing well of support; to Nina Shengold for trading manuscript pages at a crucial time and offering her own family connection to the Mexican Revolution; to Susan Richards, Martha Frankel, Abby Thomas, Gretchen Primack, Susan Sindall, and Melissa Holbrook Pierson for helping me muddle through the middle; and to my current golden writers circle: Marlene Adelstien, Pat Anderson, and Barbara Bash for giving a push toward the finish line (and helping me believe there actually *was* one).

I'm also very grateful to my sister Robin Krawitz and to Colin Sells for spectacular research support; to Audrey Couloumbis for her dream board tutorials, ongoing inspiration, and boots-on-the-ground lectures on writing craft; to Mary Louise Wilson for lifesaving porch chats and the best agent recommendation ever; to Emma Parry for taking a chance on middle-grade fiction; to editor Kelly Loughman for chasing all the bats and squirrels out of this novel's story attic; and to the rest of the Holiday House crew for their enthusiasm, skill, and a cracking good cover.

My gratitude to the Association of Jewish Libraries' Sydney Taylor Manuscript Award committee and chair Aileen Grossburg is boundless. This is a wonderfully helpful award program for writers.

And so is my appreciation for Bruce Davenport, for every kind of invaluable life support, not the least of which was the force of his belief. And finally, a huge bow of thanks to my daughter, Hannah Munson, for inspiring and thrilling me with her own creative journey.